STARS IN HER EYES

CLARE C. MARSHALL

For Liam
Follow Your Dreams!

BOOK ONE
THE SPARKSTONE SAGA

FAERY INK PRESS
faeryinkpress.com
Calgary, Alberta
aurora@faeryinkpress.com

Other books by Clare C. Marshall:

The Violet Fox
Within

PART ONE

To go home again, is that not a desire developed in the minds of intelligent, cultured beings? We who leave home at tender ages create worlds within worlds to feel an ounce of what we once felt in the arms of our mothers.

—J.G.C., from *Campbell's Multiple Verses*

PROLOGUE

The girl with the red hair comes, but she is too late.

The green serpent hides in their midst, casting long false shadows on the wall as she rears and bares her fangs.

Flashing skin and scales; the serpent and the woman are one.

The backhanded strike cracks like lightning, and her cheek stings and reddens, as if the blow were real.

Because it will be.

A gasp catches in Sunni's throat as she wakes. Her cheek is burning. There is no mark there, not yet, because everything she's seen hasn't happened yet.

Sunni throws the covers from her bare legs and pads across the cold hardwood to the bathroom. The only light comes from the shell-shaped nightlight plugged in above the vanity. A wide, tear-drop-shaped mirror hangs above the sink. Sunni can't avoid her reflection forever. She grabs the plastic cup resting on the marble counter, pours herself some water, and downs it. It won't wash away anything, not really.

The mirror reveals everything. Her blonde curls are frizzled from sleep. The ponytail she'd tied before bed is almost gone, the blue elastic band barely hanging on to a tangled clump of hair strung over her left shoulder. A young woman stares back at her with bleary green eyes. The dream is still reflected in her pupils. She watches the images over and over again, knowing that no matter how much she rubs the sleep from her eyes, no matter how much time she puts between the dream and the present moment, it won't go away. It doesn't work like that. Not with these types of dreams.

Touching the mirror with gentle fingertips, Sunni leans forward, over the vanity, and presses her forehead against her reflection. While her breath fogs the mirror, the meaning of the dream becomes clear.

Two things will come to pass.

One: the girl the Collective is searching for will arrive soon.

And two: to save her friends, Sunni must die.

CHAPTER 1

"Open the trunk, please."

Dad pops the trunk. I'm tense, even though I've got nothing to hide.

Well, that's not entirely true. I just want to get my first day over with.

The toll booth guard has a slow gait, and his footfalls go *thump . . . thump . . . thump . . . thump* in something slower than three-four time. My nerves are racing, filling in the frantic notes to the waltz the guard is creating as he walks around the car to the trunk. He's pushing around my instruments and my suitcases. *Don't touch them,* I want to say. What I'm sure is the side of my harp case scrapes against what has to be my soft keyboard covering, and I flinch.

I roll down my window. "Be careful with the instruments," I say, not wanting to come off as bitchy but at the same time not really caring. The instruments are my children.

The guard grunts something in reply and leans to the side to look at me. I decide I don't like this man. It's not his puggish face and the mole with a hair growing out of it on his right cheek that has set me off. It isn't that his teeth have the yellowy tinge of someone who has been smoking cigarettes for thirty-odd years. It's that he's staring at me as if I'm a waste of his time. As if he has better things to do than preside over the entrance of a top-secret university in the middle-of-nowhere Alberta. *It's not my fault that you have this job*, I think. *I don't want to be here either.*

Dad sticks his head out the window so that he too can make pleasant conversation. "Do you inspect everyone's trunks?"

The guard nods, then shrugs and slams the lid shut. The car shakes and Mum mutters something under her breath about the suspension.

"Is standard procedure, sir," the guard replies, but now he doesn't sound as bored as he looks. I guess he's decided we're not criminals, or maybe looking at the instruments made him think that we're worth talking to. He writes something on a yellow Post-it note, then tears it off the pad and holds it out to Dad between two sausage fingers. "Sir. Put this in your windshield and no one should give this family any trouble about parking."

He's got a strange accent I can't place. I try to hold its melody in my mind but then Mum talks and muddles my concentration. "Where's the best place to get something to eat?"

The guard looks from Mum to me. He tilts his head and appears to appraise me.

"No cafés open until noontime, ma'am," he says.

"Oh, that's a shame," Dad says, because it's barely ten in the morning. "Do you have a map of the town? Never been here before, don't want to get lost before we deposit Ingrid, you know?"

The guard's fat lips twitch a bit and he nods again and ventures to his toll booth a few feet away, to the left of the car. The large golden gate blocking our entrance to the town of Sparkstone is closed, and the thick white concrete-and-brick walls stretch into the horizon. Sparkstone is determined to keep outsiders out. Or insiders in. I wonder what secrets it holds.

"Ask him if we have to pay a toll," Mum hisses to Dad as

she peers suspiciously at the guard, who is fumbling with papers in his portapotty-sized toll booth.

"I think he would've said something if there were a toll," Dad replies.

"Well . . . Ingrid, did your acceptance package say anything about the toll booth? What about the website?" Mum twists around in her seat to look at me, panicked.

We've driven seven hours in total to get to this gate. Three hours from Calgary, a quick stop in Edmonton for the night, and now four hours this morning. Worth it, my parents think, because Sparkstone University is an upstanding institution that churns out graduates who apparently acquire positions in their fields of study all over the world. But I don't have the heart to tell them the truth: that the website is just four pages of filler text with stock images of smiling faces and small-town charming buildings; that even though the acceptance letter is curled in my fist, I don't remember applying to any institution called Sparkstone University.

"There's some change in the dash," Dad says. "Relax. He'll tell us what we need to do. You're stressing Ingrid out enough." He glances at me in the rear-view mirror. "You okay back there?"

"Yeah," I say, crumpling the wrinkled acceptance letter some more in my hand.

The guard *thump . . . thumps* back to our car. Out of habit I glance behind us. Nope, we're not holding anyone up. We're not in the big city anymore. The prairies stretch out as far as I can see. Farmland dominates the area for several kilometres but trees appear in the distance, bunched in neat clusters near run-down farmhouses and barns. The Canadian Rockies are small lumps in the horizon. When I turn around the guard is handing Dad a cartoonish map, as if we were going into a children's amusement park instead of an elite university town.

"This should tell the family everything they want to know, sir," the guard says in his funny accent.

Mum's face is disapproving as she studies the map, but she doesn't make her concerns known. My disappointment grows. Sparkstone is not cheap, and I hadn't qualified for a student loan. My parents supposedly make too much. You'd think a top-secret university would have enough money to create a more informative map instead of a mess of colourful blobs. Maybe Sparkstone is so top-secret that a map would compromise whatever is beyond that golden gate.

The guard is staring at me again with his round, dark eyes. Maybe it's my long curly red hair. No, it's not dyed, I generally have to tell people. Dark red is my natural colour. Or maybe the guy is just a creep and he only took this boring gate job so he could check out attractive young women attending the university. Maybe.

"Well," Dad says, "are we allowed in?"

Remembering himself, the guard nods and then, as an afterthought, smacks the hood of the car. It's supposed to come off as good-natured but it only makes the three of us more uncomfortable. Mum laughs nervously. I count: one second, two seconds, and then the guard also laughs, but it sounds like a woodpecker against a tree.

"Let's go," I whisper to Dad.

He inches the car forward, but the guard saunters along like a lazy hippopotamus to his cramped booth. Then he slumps down in chair and presses some buttons. Without a sound, the gate swings open from the middle. I might be imagining things, but I think the guard winks at me from behind the tinted toll booth glass.

Let me out of this car, I scream in my mind. Take me back to Calgary or send me out east to Toronto or Montreal or Halifax to some other university with my friends. But we're already past the golden gates. What could be so special that thousands of people have elected to work and learn and *live* in the middle of nowhere?

The town spills out before us. First, it introduces itself through rows of houses and streets branching off

11

the main road, probably leading to more suburbs. The houses look as if they've been built within the last ten years, and they sport fresh coats of paint in subdued whites and blues. The lawns are a rich green, and some houses even have small flower gardens. On the right, the further in we drive, more commercial streets appear, with local mum-and-pop shops. There are even some people my age walking along the sidewalks.

"This is so cute, Ingrid, take a look," Mum says, holding up the cartoonish map and comparing it to real life outside. "Let's see. There's a bakery, a mall . . . some cafés, a pub, not that you'll need to know that, right? Grocery store . . . though your residence fees included a meal plan. Remember that woman who called yesterday, said she was from the Sparkstone registration office? Gosh, I can't remember her name. Anyway, they said that almost everything you eat is grown within Sparkstone itself. Isn't that amazing? They even have a garden on campus that students can tend!"

That phone call was the only one we'd received from Sparkstone, and Mum had drilled whoever was on the line for at least an hour with questions about the town and the university. Both my parents had been sceptical about sending me, their only child, away to a place they knew nothing about until that phone call. I guess the woman she'd talked to had alleviated most of her fears, which is kind of a feat in and of itself.

"Sounds like you should enrol with me then," I remark with a smirk.

"I don't think I can afford two university tuitions. Sorry, Margaret," Dad says.

Mum laughs and continues to study the map. Actually, she is right. The town is kind of cute. I forget the expansive ocean of green grass surrounding us beyond the wall when I see the prim white townhouses lining the roads, when the people smile and wave at our car as they walk their dogs, and when the smell of freshly baked bread wafts through the air. The bakery is on the left, and there's a line out the door.

As we draw closer to the centre of town and pass the cafés and the pub and the mall, the buildings morph again. Tall, large, historic-looking structures made of stone make me wonder how old Sparkstone University is. *Not that old,* I think. Based on the way the city has been laid out so far, with the houses in grids like the new houses popping up in Calgary, and the commercial buildings all in one place, Sparkstone seems to have been a planned building initiative. As we approach a roundabout and drive into Sparkstone's campus, I read the labels: MacLeod Hall, Hynes House. I search for years when the buildings may have been constructed, or maybe even a large plaque explaining whom the buildings are named after, but find nothing.

When the school counsellor told me that I'd been accepted to Sparkstone University, I told her I'd never applied to a college by that name. She'd looked at me—*me,* Ingrid Stanley—as if I were an idiot, her bug eyes even rounder behind her thick glasses. Sparkstone University doesn't accept *applicants,* she'd told me, me with a 98 percent average, me the valedictorian, me the soon-to-be award winner of every single plaque and bursary the high school could possibly throw at a seventeen-year-old girl with an aptitude for music, science, and humanities. Sparkstone University sends *scouts* to high schools to look for bright young students who show promise. She was smug when she'd told me this. I guess her claim to fame was that she'd talked to the Sparkstone scout for a few hours about me and my grades.

I was angry. She'd passed along my school records to Sparkstone without even consulting me. That day, facing the guidance counsellor, I was the closest I've ever come to standing up to a teacher and telling her off. But I didn't do that. Not because I was afraid. Because I had a reputation to uphold. I never got angry at teachers. I never got seriously angry with my parents. I never raised my voice to either of them. I knew how to choose my battles, I'd tell myself, but really, I just wanted to get through high school and hurry up to the part of my life where I'd be making a difference in the world. And Sparkstone seemed like a good opportunity for someone who worked hard and cared about getting a good job. And maybe the guidance counsellor was right and Sparkstone was the kind of place where young, bright minds were collected and cultivated. I might even find some people who liked learning for fun.

So instead of protesting, I mumbled a thank-you to the counsellor. And a week later, I got the official acceptance letter in the mail. I crumple it some more in my hand as I watch some maple trees blow in a gentle breeze. A couple of students are lying in a patch of grass beside a building, reading books and probably discussing them. I catch the title on one of the covers: Plato's *Republic*.

Maybe I'm riding into something that I shouldn't be. I could still decline, make a fuss, tell my parents I've made a huge mistake and beg for them to drive seven hours back to Calgary. But if there's one thing I'm not, it's a quitter. And if there's one thing I have more than anything else, it's curiosity. So I will stand in the fire and see what this supposedly elite university for super smart people can offer, and I will fire back.

Besides, I can't go back. I have no backup plan. I applied for three other universities across the country but they all rejected my applications with polite but terse letters. Rejected me, with all of my grades and extracurriculars. I was a shoo-in for any place, my parents had always told me. And yet, it was Sparkstone that *had* to have me.

Which only made me more intrigued.

And nervous.

I tap a melody out on my shins: "If Ever You Were Mine," a Celtic ballad I'm fond of playing on the piano. I relax as the familiar notes play in my head. Mum's from Cape Breton, in Nova Scotia, and that's where my aptitude for music comes from, she says. It's thousands of miles away and she's not really musical herself, but the music found me anyway—piano lessons since I was eight through the Royal Conservatory and yearly summer trips to the Gaelic College in Cape Breton. I started on the Celtic harp when I was eleven. It's in the trunk, along with my keyboard. I hope the creepy guard didn't bang them up too much with his inspection.

Dad slows the car and pulls into a small parking lot in front of one of the historic buildings. Mum and Dad are arguing about whether or not it's the right place.

"This is what it says in the legend, Rita House, for registration," Mum says, pointing at a grey blob on the map.

So we're here. I suck in a deep breath. Mum notices my nerves and reaches back to squeeze my knee. "You'll do fine, Ingrid! We'll come in with you and make sure you're settled."

I smile at her. "Thanks, Mum."

As soon as Dad cuts the engine, the front door of Rita House opens and a tall, thin woman emerges. Long silvery-blonde hair runs straight down her back, but she doesn't look a day over thirty. A warm smile lights up her flawless face as I step out of the car, and she glides towards me. She extends her arms, as if to draw me into a hug, but instead rests her hands on my shoulders.

"Hello, Ingrid," she says, her voice like creamy honey with a hint of a foreign accent. Spanish, maybe?

Mum approaches the woman, clutching her purse tightly. "Are you . . . oh sorry, I spoke with a woman on the phone yesterday . . . I forget her name."

"I am Ms. Grace Agailya. And yes, Mrs. Stanley, I did speak with you yesterday," Ms. Agailya says, releasing her gentle grip on my shoulders. She shakes Mum's hand. "Very nice to meet you." Her pale blue eyes flit to me. "We have been looking forward to your arrival."

She looks more like an elf than someone who works at a university, I think as I study Ms. Agailya's frail but

15

graceful form. Her long white skirt flutters between her legs with the calming breeze.

"Are you in charge of registration?" Dad asks as he shuts the car door.

"I am the head housemistress here at Sparkstone University," she explains. "It's my responsibility to keep an eye on all students and make sure they're comfortable here. I'll help you with whatever you need. You must be tired from your long journey." She smiles and looks at Dad sympathetically, as if he'd pulled us and all the luggage in a rickshaw instead of having driven for seven hours. "Do you have any suitcases you need help with?"

"More than enough suitcases," Dad mutters.

I'm not really sure it's a good idea to let the frail-looking woman help with my heavy bags and instruments, but Dad is already unloading the trunk, and maybe it would be rude to say no to her, since she so kindly asked. I remove my harp case first because I don't trust anyone else to carry it, while Dad points to one of my smaller bags containing notebooks and my laptop. "Uh, sure, Ms. Agailya, just grab the—"

Ms. Agailya reaches for one of the large, heavy suitcases that contains most of my clothes. I'm about to tell her to leave that one for Dad but she lifts it up as if it's full of feathers.

"I think there're some wheels on it, and a slide-out handle if you need help," I say as I yank one of the smaller suitcases from beneath the pile of stuff in the back. The wheels scrape against the pavement as I gain control of the unwieldy valise.

"I'm fine," Ms. Agailya says with a smile. "I'm stronger than I look."

"Yeah, seems like," I mutter. I wonder if there's an easier, more graceful way to lug my suitcases and instruments to where we're supposed to be. I decide that my harp is the only thing I can carry and leave the smaller suitcase for Mum and Dad to worry about.

"Come," says Ms. Agailya, gesturing to a large, three-storey Edwardian building across the street. "We'll worry about registration and such later. Let me show you to your room."

There's no parking on the other side of the road, so Mum and Dad take what they can carry and lock the door while Ms. Agailya strides across the road without looking—not that there's much traffic anyway. Crisp-white window frames encircle the blemish-free glass, but the brick finishing looks as though it's seen more than its fair share of harsh winters. Tall maple trees protect the historic building with their wide, reaching branches: three on each side, and at least four in the back.

"This is Rogers Hall," Ms. Agailya explains as I run to catch up with her. "The cafeteria is on the main level, and then above that we have a handful of classrooms, studies, and temporary residences for guests and new students. Over there"—she thumbs behind her, where our car is parked—"is the main girls' residence, Rita House, and the other girls' residence, Raylene House, beside it. Across from Raylene House, to the left of Rogers Hall, is Morris House and behind Rogers Hall is Hynes House. Morris House and Hynes House are the male residences. While as an institution we are fairly liberal, we do have rather strict rules governing opposite sex visitors at inappropriate hours of the night."

"That shouldn't be a problem for me." I feel lame admitting this. I only had one boyfriend in high school, and it only lasted a month. Between music lessons, studying for school, being on the student council, learning to play anything remotely nerdy on the piano, and, let's face it, watching *Doctor Who* and reading *Star Wars* fan fiction on the Internet, I didn't have a lot of time for a boyfriend. Or rather, guys I knew didn't seem to have a lot of time for me.

Approaching the residence and looking up makes my move to the remote university town of Sparkstone feel so real. I'm growing up. I'm making a fresh start. Maybe, somewhere within these walls are people like me. People who will laugh and nod knowingly at my *Star Wars* and *Doctor Who* and *Battlestar Galactica* references. People who, when they want to know something, actually take the time to look it up and who read for *fun* instead of stumbling around life blindly relying on the smart kids to push them through difficult situations. I'm not going to be the smart kid anymore. I'm going to be in a sea of them. This both terrifies and excites me. Mostly terrifies. What if I'm not smart enough to even be here? What if my acceptance here is a mistake, and I really, truly have nowhere to go?

I gulp. I guess I'll just have to fake it until I make it.

I walk ahead of Ms. Agailya and reach for the double doors. They're made of reflective steel that, unlike the brick, looks brand new. My fingers clasp the protruding handle and—

OW!

A computerized female voice speaks softly from hidden speakers. "DNA match confirmed. Blood type, O. Welcome to Sparkstone, Ingrid Louise Stanley."

CHAPTER 2

There is a red dot in the middle of my index finger. It stings like crazy. *Did the* door *just take my blood sample?*

"Sorry, Ingrid. I should have warned you. Standard policy," Ms. Agailya says as she approaches the doors. "We take a blood sample from each new student for security purposes. It's used to formulate your key card, which allows you to access your permanent residence, your classes, and the recreational facilities."

This sounds highly illegal to me. "But how? I just touched the door. Is it going to take my parents' blood samples too if they touch the door?"

"We have some of the most brilliant minds here at Sparkstone. The software scans each fingerprint, determines its relation to a current student, professor, or other employee, and allows him or her to enter."

"I see." My finger has stopped stinging, but I'm afraid to go inside. "But the voice said DNA match *confirmed.* So you must have already had my DNA on file."

"Yes, well." Her pale face colours. "Our scouts are quite thorough when researching potential students. But we have to make sure . . . "

"Ms. Agailya? Would you mind taking this?" Mum calls from behind the car. She sounds out of breath as she lugs

Clare C. Marshall

one of my suitcases from the trunk.

"You may go inside, Ingrid. We'll be right behind you," Ms. Agailya says.

When she turns around, I bunch up the fabric of my sleeves into my right hand and open the door. No alarms sound, and the door opens easily. Maybe the security system can read my DNA through my clothes. I shudder. *Hopefully that's the last of the creepiness in this town.*

I'm in a lobby. There's a set of stairs immediately to my right, and a security desk to the left. It's occupied by another tubby guard, wearing an orange construction vest, who looks just as disinterested in protecting the school as the guard at the gate. He lifts his eyes from the *Canadian Living* magazine, looks me up and down, and then gets up from his chair. He grabs a black box from the desk, tucks it and the magazine under his arm, and disappears up the stairs. I keep a careful eye on him as he ascends. The ceiling is so high on this floor that I can see part of a hallway on the second floor. There are another few steps in front of me, leading down into a reception area. I smell bacon and eggs, and my stomach growls. The cafeteria must be somewhere close by.

Out the door windows, I see Mum and Dad struggling with my suitcases. *I should go help them.*

Light footsteps descend the steps beside me and stop suddenly. "No . . . "

I frown and turn around. Before me is a girl, about my age, dressed in green pyjama pants, a long T-shirt, and a white housecoat. Her curly blonde hair poofs out from her freckled, flushed face, and she's a bit out of breath. Her gaze bores into mine; she's staring at me as if she knows me.

"Hello," I say, setting my harp case down carefully on the tiled floor.

The girl parts her lips to speak, but nothing comes out.

"Do you . . . do you need help?" It seems like a stupid thing to ask, but I don't know what to make of her behaviour.

20

After a minute, the girl shakes her head of her intense stare and says, "Sorry. I just . . . I just woke up." She grins, showing off the dimples on either side of her mouth. She runs her fingers through her curls to straighten them, but they just twist and frizz back as they were. "I was just makin' sure you felt welcome. My first day, I didn't have anyone. Well, except Misty I guess." She laughs a little. Her voice is filled with a Texas twang. "Are you needin' any help with your bags?"

"I think we've got them, thanks." I lengthen the handle of the suitcase again. "What's your name?"

"I'm Sunni. Sunni Harris."

She grins again, and there's so much warmth in it that I can almost smell fresh country grass and homemade pies and cookies.

"I'm Ingrid," I say.

"I know."

"You . . . know?"

Sunni bites her lip as embarrassment colours her freckled face. "Well . . . I guess, yeah, I do know. I saw your file in Ms. Agailya's office when I was in there, and she deals a lot with . . . "

She trails off as Dad, holding a bag, opens the door and holds it open for Mum and Ms. Agailya. Mum wheels in another large suitcase while Ms. Agailya carries a small travel bag. Dad manages to slip inside before the door closes on him completely.

"Ingrid, honey, your keyboard is still in the car. I'll go back and get it," Dad says as he sets one of my suitcases down.

"You need any help?" I ask.

"No, I'll be right back."

Dad leaves and Ms. Agailya is about to go up the steps when she notices Sunni gripping the stair railing as if her legs are about to give out.

"Sunni Harris," Ms. Agailya says, looking surprised. "You're out here in your pyjamas. Is anything the matter?"

"Oh . . . no," Sunni replies. She's got a sheepish look on

her face, and if I were her, I'd be embarrassed. "Just saw her comin' in and thought I'd like to say hello, is all. I can show Ingrid to her room, if you're busy, Ms. Agailya."

"No, Sunni, you don't have to worry about that. Thank you, though. Breakfast ends in a half hour. You might want to hurry or you'll miss it."

Sunni curls her hands and sticks them in her armpits, for warmth. "I already ate, actually."

"Good. Ingrid, we shouldn't keep Sunni from her morning routine." She starts up the stairs.

Mum follows her, and I give Sunni one last smile. "It was nice to meet you."

"Yeah, same to you," Sunni says. "Look, one thing before you go." Her gaze flickers up to Mum and Ms. Agailya, who are disappearing down the second-floor hallway, and to Dad, who is inching closer to the door with my keyboard carried across his shoulder, and then settles on me again. "Don't eat the food, if you can help it."

I frown. "Is it really that bad?"

Her cheeriness has been replaced with the solemnity of someone who has seen the darker face of the world. "Yeah. There's this café down the road. Eat there, it's . . . it's still not great, but it's better than everythin' you can eat here."

I don't want to say so, but I'm pretty sure Dad already bought the meal plan. You have to, if you're going to live in residence. And if you're attending Sparkstone University, you have to live in residence.

"I'm sure I'll get along fine," I say.

Sunni's smile is grim. "You probably will, yeah."

Something in Sunni's green eyes glue me in place. There are words she can't say swirling around in her irises. A plea: *please, listen to me.* I place a firm foot on the step. I have to go. Mum and Ms. Agailya are already out of sight and I don't want to get lost on the first day.

The door opens a crack. Dad is trying to get in with the keyboard. I hold the door as he strolls inside unsteadily, and again, refuses my offer to help. He nods a hello to Sunni on his way up the stairs.

"It was nice to meet you," I say to Sunni, lifting my hand in an awkward wave. "I'll see you later?"

"You count on it." Her smile is more genuine, more relaxed now.

I pick up my harp case and race up the stairs after my parents and Ms. Agailya. I turn around to catch a glimpse of Sunni again but she's already gone. Despite her weird preferences about the school's food, I can see her being my first friend. *Maybe there's a place for me here after all.*

There's a hallway off to the left, and my parents are at the end of it, waiting. The carpet floor is worn, the lights hanging on the wall are dim, and there are faint scratches on the walls, as if someone had dragged her fingernails across the panelling. I can't help but picture some poor student being pulled against her will to her room. University dorms are closet spaces at best. I prepare myself for the worst.

"My apologies, Ingrid," Ms. Agailya says as she produces a key from her breast pocket. "My staff are not yet finished preparing your room, as we didn't know your individual tastes. This room is only temporary."

The key clicks sharply in the lock and the door opens, revealing an outdated hotel room. Flowery wallpaper, flowery bedspread, dark green carpet. It's old, but it doesn't matter because it's huge. Twice the size of my bedroom at home, at least. The bed is on the back wall and it has a circular mattress. I've never slept on a bed shaped like a circle before. Everything looks slightly used—the four-drawer, wide oak dresser over to the left by the bathroom door, the scratched, bruised nightstand to the right of the bed, and the long, heavy, off-white curtains on the back window— but nothing smells old or musty. It's antique. I don't want to touch anything for fear of breaking something.

"This is only a temporary room?" I ask in disbelief.

"Yes. Again, my apologies," Ms. Agailya says. She hands

me a spare key from her pocket. "Keep it safe. There's a charge for a replacement key if you lose it."

I think it's strange that a high-tech school has physical keys for its doors, but if they didn't have my blood to make into a key card in the first place, I guess the key is necessary.

Dad whistles as he drops one of my suitcases onto the thick carpet. "Maybe we should get a room here. What do you say to that, Ingrid?"

"Oh, Craig, stop," Mum says, hitting him playfully on the arm.

I flop backwards onto my new bed and immediately melt into the mattress. I don't think I've ever lain on something so comfy. Sleep will come easily for me tonight. My eyes already feel heavy. "Do I have classes today?"

"Yes. After you're settled, we'll go to the registrar and sort out your major."

"Ugh," I say, rolling over and basking in the softness of the bed. "I could fall asleep right now!"

Dad chuckles as Mum checks out the room, probably inspecting it for cleanliness. I breathe in the scent of the quilt. It smells as fresh as the day the artisan put the finishing stitches in its intricate twirling-flower design. Large room, beautiful campus—this school has money. More money than any other university in Canada, maybe in all of North America. This is luxury I could get used to.

"Ms. Agailya? Ms Agailya!"

A young man's voice—thick with a British accent of some kind—echoes through the hallway. He scampers into the room: six-foot-one, lanky build, cropped curly dark hair. He sports a leather jacket that looks as if it's seen more than its share of action. I sit up instantly and mind my skirt and fix my hair. Guys in leather jackets can't be ignored, under any circumstances. He smiles at me and his eyes are kind, and fiercely green. My grin betrays my pounding heart.

His gaze slides to my harp case, lying against the wall. He jerks his thumb at it. "You're a musician?"

The first thing out of my mouth? "I like your leather jacket."

His grin widens. "I like your leather boots. Knee-highs?"

"Knee-high, steel-toed, real leather. Got them for my birthday. From my mum." I'm so giddy I'm practically bouncing on the bed. "They're my faves."

Ms. Agailya is not impressed. "Ethan Millar. You know you're not allowed on this floor. It's for girls only."

"Sorry." He face reddens, but I'm not sorry. I don't think he is either, because he's still smiling like a boy whose hand has been caught in the cookie jar. He hands her a folded note. "Professor Jadore wanted me to give you this."

Ms. Agailya's eyes sweep quickly over the note before she refolds it and sticks it in her breast pocket. "It seems I have a matter to take care of. Mr. and Mrs. Stanley, allow me to escort you to registration and we can get you sorted there. Ingrid, your tutorial starts in half an hour— normally I'd ask you to come to the registrar's office, but we don't like our new students, especially late arrivals, missing their first tutorials. Perhaps, Ethan, you could show her to her tutorial room?"

"Sure." He turns his half-smile to me again and I melt a little bit more. "Did you need to unpack first?"

"No, I guess I can do it later," I reply. "I don't want to be late on my first day. What about registering my major? And how do I know what classes I'm taking, if I've never signed up for any?"

"Maybe Ethan will be able to explain how we do things here at Sparkstone. Normally, I would, but . . . " She opens the door and gestures to Mum and Dad. "I'm sorry, but I really must be going, and Ingrid must not be late for her tutorial."

"Who is her tutor?" Ethan asks.

"Put her with Professor Jadore for now, and we can re-evaluate once her project for this semester has been

25

decided. Room 216." She clears her throat. "After my matter has been attended to, perhaps, Mr. and Mrs. Stanley, you would appreciate a tour of the grounds?"

"Well . . . " Mum is hesitant. "We've got to get back to the city before it gets too late."

"Of course, of course. I'll leave you to say your goodbyes, then."

Ms. Agailya steps gracefully into the hallway and leaves the door ajar. This bothers me more than I let on, but before I can dwell on it, Mum is hugging me so tightly that the air is forced from my lungs.

"Whenever you need us," she says, "just call."

Her tears stain my cheeks. Ethan leans against the wall next to my harp. I'm embarrassed; he shouldn't have to witness this private moment between me and my family. I stay strong because I don't want to cry in front of a stranger, especially since the stranger is a cute guy. Finally Mum lets go and Dad comes forward, smiling thinly to conceal his pride and his fear of letting go, and hugs me goodbye. Mum and Dad are the only family I have, and I'm the only child they have. I can't disappoint them.

"We'll visit as soon as we can," Mum promises, wiping her tears with her coat sleeve.

I nod. "Have a safe trip home."

And then like that, they're walking away from me, out the door and into the hallway. The light catches Ms. Agailya's silvery-blue eyes and makes them shine like precious jewels. With a last wave, they disappear from sight, leaving the door open.

I take a deep breath and let it go to dispel the anxiety and the sadness welling within my stomach.

"Um, we'd better get going," Ethan says finally, stepping away from the wall. "You don't want to be late for Jadore's tutorial."

I grab my backpack from among the scattered luggage—my laptop is in it, as well as a notebook and some pens—and follow Ethan out of my new room. "Is Professor

26

Jadore strict or mean or something?"

Ethan grimaces. "Well . . . most of the students don't really like her. She's one of those people who never seems to be happy about anything."

"Oh." I lock the door with Ms. Agailya's key and slip it into my skirt pocket. Together, we start down the hallway. "Will she be my only . . . tutor . . . then? What about lectures, or classes?"

He grins. "We don't really have them."

"What? But how—?"

"It's almost all independent study in whatever field you choose. In the tutorials, there are small groups of six or seven or eight people and you discuss what you're doing. They're mixed so that no student in the same tutorial is studying the same thing."

This isn't what I had expected. I slow my stride. "You mean the students have to pay to go to school where they just do independent projects and talk about them? Sounds like anyone could do that themselves."

"True," Ethan admits, shoving his hands into his jeans pockets. "Except that at the end of the semester, the projects are reviewed and graded by top people in your field. And usually, the best of the best projects attract attention, and it's easy for Sparkstone grads to get jobs that way, or at the very least, opportunities they wouldn't get otherwise." He shrugs. "So, what are you thinking of studying?"

Music, I almost say. I massage my piano fingers. They itch to play. I had considered taking a year off to teach music or applying for a college or university where I could continue to study and learn, but my parents had strongly recommended that I choose something else. Something more "traditional" to study.

"Psychology, maybe," I say instead. "Maybe sociology or another social science. I guess I haven't really decided yet."

"That's all right. You've got two majors to pick. Just decide one soon and you can pick the other one later."

"Two majors? Everyone has two majors?"

"Yeah. Sparkstone's different than other universities." He runs a hand through his short hair.

"You can say that again," I mutter.

"Ahh, it's not so bad," Ethan says. His hand lingers over my shoulder, as if he's about to reassure me, but he withdraws it quickly with an awkward smile. "Just as long as you're not a procrastinator. Last semester I left my art collection to the last minute. I spent three straight days painting, drawing . . . I went in to meet the woman evaluating my pieces and honest to God, I can't even remember how the meeting went, I was so tired. I probably looked wrecked."

He laughs at himself, and I find myself laughing too. We descend the stairs to the lobby area again. There's no sign of Sunni. *She must be on her way to class by now.* Ethan opens the door and leads me across the street, around Rita House. The grass smells as if it was mowed yesterday and reminds me of the pleasant lime-green tones of a song in E major. Some students find shelter beneath randomly placed maple trees, where they read books and type on laptops, while others like us trudge towards a brick building across the curved roundabout road. The gold-plated sign above the double-doored entrance reads MacLeod Hall.

"Don't you find it odd that they never explained all this?" I ask as I breathe in the brisk September air. "That it's not on their website, or brochures? That they don't advertise at the university fairs in high schools? Why wouldn't they want people to know about this beautiful little town?"

Ethan shrugs again, his leather jacket making a comforting rustling sound. "I suppose it's strange. But Sparkstone has its own way of doing things, you see. There's all this secretive business but really it's just to keep the ones who don't deserve to be here out, and those who are worthy to be here in."

I raise an eyebrow. "And who just *is* worthy of being here?"

"Well, you must know yourself, being chosen." His half-smile is back. "The smartest, the brightest in their fields. Sparkstone handpicks them from across the world." He points a thumb at his chest. "I'm a second-year. Was surprised last year that I got accepted to a university in Canada, without even applying, not a visa on me either. But, they got that all sorted, and here I am."

"Where are you from exactly?" I'm terrible at discerning accents. My face heats—hopefully he doesn't think I'm stupid for not being able to identify his accent, after going on about how only the brightest are accepted to Sparkstone.

"Outside of London. There aren't many of us Brits here."

I'm about to ask him more about his English heritage, and if he enjoys British science-fiction TV shows, but as soon as we step inside MacLeod Hall, I'm overcome with the feeling that I'm in high school again. A narrow lobby makes a sharp left, widens, and turns into a corridor. Lockers line the wall to my right, while floor-to-ceiling windows let in the late-morning sunlight to my left as we stroll down the hallway. A pair of double doors hides another wing and some stairs to another level. There are three classroom doors interspersed between the lockers. There's no one else in the hallway except us—the students I saw before have been swallowed up by the classrooms—and it feels like the calm before the storm.

"Anyway, Room 216 is there," Ethan says, pointing to the classroom door closest to us. "I have to go, or I'll be late for my own tutorial."

"Oh. I didn't mean to make you late." I clutch the straps of my backpack, feeling silly, not knowing what to do with my hands, not knowing what this guy expects of me, wanting to disappear but stay at the same time.

Ethan starts to head down the hallway towards the exit, but his gaze remains fixed on me. "I'll see you later then, yeah?"

"Yes, definitely!" Inside, I'm cursing myself. That sounded too eager. "I mean, yeah, that . . . that would be cool."

He smiles and shakes his head. "It's my accent, isn't it. Always messes with the ladies' heads. Makes them . . . " He trails off, and his face turns a shade as dark as my hair. "How abouts I give you a proper tour after? That is, unless you're busy unpacking or something. I'd help with that too but I don't think Ms. Agailya would like me in the women's dorms again without permission."

"I'd like that. The tour, that is."

"All right then. I'll meet you here after tutorial, yeah?"

"Sounds good."

He waves goodbye. I face the classroom door. Through its tiny window, I see chairs arranged in a semicircle. There are already students in there. I should really go inside.

But . . .

I glance over my shoulder, to see if Ethan is stealing one last look at me. He's not. The hall is empty. Oh well. It's only the first day, and I've only known him for fifteen minutes. There's no way—

I step forward and bump into someone who wasn't there before. Startled, I lose my balance as my feet get tripped up in something long, thin, and hard. The floor rushes up to meet me.

CHAPTER 3

My head strikes the floor and pain radiates through my body.

First thought: *At least Ethan isn't here to see me fall.*

Second thought: *I shouldn't have worn these gigantic leather boots today.*

Third thought: *Ethan did seem to like my boots though.*

I groan and climb to my feet as I wipe off my skirt and check for bruises. No major damage, except for my pride. A woman stands in my periphery. I feel her watching me, silently, unapologetically.

"I didn't see you there, sorry," I say. I just want to get into the classroom now. Hopefully none of the students saw me fall. That would be embarrassing.

"I did not see you either," the woman replies.

I frown. "How could you not see me when—"

Oh.

I look up at the person responsible for my fall. The six-foot-tall woman is dressed in a green business suit that brings out her skin's copper hues, but she also carries a long, thin black cane. That's what I must have tripped over. Reflective sunglasses obscure most of her face and mirror my surprise. Guilt drives into my chest like a slippery knife.

"I'm sorry," I say, covering my mouth. "I didn't know you were . . . " It seems like a bad word to say. *"Blind."*

"And I don't believe we've met." Her voice is a bit gravelly and contains an accent, maybe German? The woman clears her throat. "You are the new student?"

"Yes. I'm Ingrid Stanley." I stick out a hand but then think better of it. "I was just going to my tutorial."

"Room 216?" the woman asks, knocking her cane against the door. "You are in my tutorial, then. I am Professor Jadore."

I clear my throat and think about what Ethan had said about her. "Nice to meet you."

"In the future, Ingrid, I prefer my students to be on time, sitting in the tutorial room before I arrive." She taps her cane once on the floor. Through the window, I see the students inside looking out at me. I blush. "Just because I'm blind doesn't mean I don't know you aren't there."

Meekly, I nod, and then remember her condition at the last minute. "Yes, Professor."

"Good."

It's unsettling to look at her face. Something about not being able to see her eyes makes Professor Jadore a hard woman to read. I'm about to help her with the door but she finds the knob just fine. Of course, she probably does this every day! Tucking a stray lock of hair behind my ear, I follow the professor into the classroom.

There are ten chairs in the semicircle but only eight students present. There are no desks. My attention is captured by a hand frantically waving in the air—it's Sunni. She's looking more presentable now, dressed in a turquoise shirt with fluffy sleeves and clean, dark skinny jeans. The dark shadows beneath her eyes persist, though they don't affect her cheery disposition. I sit down in the empty chair beside her.

I part my lips to say something to her, but she shakes her head slightly. She points at her notebook, where she's scrawled: *I had a feeling you would be here with us.*

Us? Before I can ask, Jadore's cane taps the floor twice and any chatter in the room ceases immediately. She finds her seat facing the semicircle, feeling the back of the chair to ensure its existence, and then sits. The cane rests across her lap. She curls one hand around it, as if she intends to use it to strike at any moment. "We'll keep this meeting to under a half hour, since I know you are behind on your projects. And I know some of you haven't started your projects yet."

I feel a lump in my throat. I'd forgotten this semester started almost a month ago, during the first week of August. We had no idea—the acceptance letter had been vague about the semester's start date, and unless you're already a current student, communicating with Sparkstone seems next to impossible. If Ms. Agailya hadn't called yesterday, Mum and Dad would've waited another week to drive me up here.

Each student gives Jadore an update about his or her project. The first is an Asian girl named Jia, and she's writing a paper about child abuse and the abuse of women and comparing it to the treatment of women and children in ancient cultures. Next to her, a tall, muscular black guy named Wil talks about something complicated involving computer engineering and mathematics. He polishes the razor-thin frames of his glasses as Professor Jadore advises him on the finer points of a particular mathematical theory. I have no idea what Jadore's speciality is as far as academics goes but I figure that she must be well versed in a lot of different subjects to advise everyone in the room.

I'm in awe of the variety of projects happening in such a small, sleepy town. I hope that I can come up with a project that sounds half as smart as what Jadore and the other students are talking about. I have to impress them if I want to fit in.

The girl sitting between Wil and Sunni is next. She smacks her gum and plays with her stretched earlobe.

Pierced septum, pierced eyebrow—I wonder if her tongue is pierced as well, and if it's even safe to chew gum with a pierced tongue. She sits with one foot perched on the seat while the other swings impatiently back and forth.

"Misty. Where are you at with your project?" Jadore asks.

Her eyes, encased in heavy mascara and shadow, flicker up in a silent challenge. They make her light skin look deathly pale. I'm not sure if she'll respond. If she weren't chewing her gum so loudly, she might be able to get away with pretending to be absent.

"It's comin' along," she says, snapping her gum again. "Doin' more research, just like you said."

"Good." Jadore's long, painted nails drum across her cane. "But I expect more of you, Misty. Your analysis of the romance languages last term was not worthy of a Sparkstone student."

Misty shrugs. "I'll try harder, I guess."

"You will."

The edge in Jadore's voice makes it clear that her authority won't be challenged. Beside me, Sunni stiffens. Misty ignores Jadore's remark and pulls part of her gum out of her mouth, creating a long string.

Jadore moves on. "Sunni?"

"Yes, Professor?" Sunni replies. Her voice wavers slightly.

"Tell me about your analysis of the Venus flytrap and the prey that manage to escape it. Have the beetles that escaped shown any sign of intelligence that the others did not? You were running several experiments last week. How are they progressing?"

She steals a glance at me before replying. Her cheery demeanour seems to vanish under Jadore's scrutiny. "Actually . . . Professor . . . I spent the past few days workin' on somethin' else."

Jadore tilts her head. If not for her sunglasses, I would have guessed she was looking directly at Sunni. "Something else?"

"Um . . . yes, Professor. See, while I was doin' some

research in the library a few days ago, I came across this website, and there was some information on this guy. Maybe . . . maybe it's not important."

"Perhaps not. But if it is pulling your attention away from your project, you must report that."

Sunni's fingers play with a loose thread on the stitching of her jeans. "Yes, Professor."

"Tell me what you've been studying instead of the Venus flytrap, Sunni."

Jadore's command cannot be ignored. A pang of fear twists around my spine as Sunni answers in the smallest, mousiest voice. "Joseph G. Campbell."

The name seems to strike a chord with Jadore. Her back straightens. "Joseph G. Campbell?"

"Yes. He's a theoretical physicist—or was, I'm not sure if he's still alive, and, uh, anyway, he had some interestin' theories about"—Sunni looks to Misty and Jia for support—"um . . . somethin' called *multiverses*."

"I am familiar with Joseph G. Campbell's work." Jadore's response is slow and deliberate. "And I know it has nothing to do with biology, or insect psychology, or any kind of psychology."

"Yes . . . I know . . . I was just . . . I just found it interestin', is all."

"If everything you found interesting was included in your study, Sunni Harris, the world would not have enough paper to print and publish it. Keep your focus, and you will do well."

Sunni leans back in her chair and plays with her fingernails. "Yes, Professor Jadore."

"One more question. On what website did you come across Joseph G. Campbell's work?"

Sunni freezes. Her bright green eyes grow wide. "Well . . . uh . . . it was just a footnote on Wikipedia, for some book, that happened to be in the library." She bites her lip, as if she's already said too much.

"A Joseph G. Campbell book here, in our library?" Jadore

raises a thin, sculpted eyebrow. "His written works are rare and out of print, and difficult to find. What treatise was it?"

"I ... I don't remember ... " Sunni looks to me for help, but I've never even heard of this Joseph G. Campbell and would be no use even if I wanted to help her.

Jia speaks up. Her voice is quiet, like Sunni's, but carries the maturity of a wise sage. "Excuse me, Professor. I was there. I was helping Sunni that day. The book was called *Campbell's Multiple Verses* and we only looked for it for ten minutes. It was very hard to find much information about this man online, and Sunni was just curious about him."

"I see. So you didn't find the book?"

"No, Professor," Jia replies. "We went back to our respective studies."

Jadore seems to chew on this for a moment. "Very well. Sunni, I expect a more thorough update from you tomorrow."

"Yes, Professor," Sunni says softly.

Jadore looks around the circle and then speaks, her tone unchanged. "Ingrid. I hope that you have gotten a sense of what we expect here at Sparkstone. Have you any idea what you would like to study this semester?"

"Um." I clear my throat. Clear and concise, that's what Jadore seems to want in an answer. "Something to do with psychology. Or music."

"You are a musician?"

"A . . . pianist, actually. And a harpist. I have my Grade 9 piano from the Royal Conservatory, and I just passed my Grade 4 in harp, with first class honours."

This actually makes Jadore smile. "You will make a promising addition to this tutorial, I feel. I look forward to your updates."

A sigh of relief escapes me. Good. I've impressed the professor. Even Sunni is smiling at me. I won't be labelled as stupid or not smart enough, hopefully. "Thank you."

I quietly take out my notebook from my backpack and make some notes about potential majors and project ideas. After another ten minutes or so of Jadore questioning the other students, we are dismissed. Some students, like Misty, leap from their chairs and leave the room as quickly as possible. Sunni lingers, waiting for Jia and Wil. Jadore remains frozen, like a statue, and stares out the window with her blind, shaded eyes. There's nothing left for me to do, so I head for the door.

"Hey, Ingrid," Sunni says. She follows me into the hallway, with Jia and Wil not too far behind. "So you're settled in, then?"

"They gave me a temporary room, yeah," I reply. I wonder if I should ask her about the blood samples and why she told me not to eat the food. I decide this might be too weird to mention out of the blue. "The room is pretty nice, but I'm looking forward to seeing what my actual room looks like. They say they customize it to your tastes?"

"Yeah." Sunni bobs her head and smiles, but her eyes are saying something different again, as they were when I met her in the lobby. She touches my arm with her warm fingers. "Listen. I know what it's like to be new and not know anyone, so if you're needin' help, or if you're needin' someone to give you a tour . . ."

I blush. "Oh. Well, someone already offered to give me a tour."

"Who?" she asks.

"Um, this guy named Ethan. I met him when I arrived."

"Ethan Millar? He's on my floor," Wil interjects. "Nice guy."

"He's very cute," Sunni adds. The sparkle is back in her eyes.

"I thought he had a girlfriend," Jia says.

Wil shakes his head. "That girl Kimberly? No, they're just friends."

"How do *you* know?" Jia nudges him lightly on the arm,

and a brief, awkward silence descends upon the group. Wil smiles a bit, adjusts his glasses, and says nothing.

"I just met him. He offered to show me around," I say, shrugging, hoping that I don't seem *too* interested in him.

"You shouldn't trust everyone you meet."

I turn around. It's Misty. I hadn't even realized she'd been standing behind us the whole time. She bites off part of her thumbnail, painted black, and spits it out on the floor. Her stare challenges me to react to her behaviour.

Sunni just smiles and squeezes Misty's arm. "I'm sure Ethan's fine. Besides, Ingrid can trust us."

Even Misty softens a little at Sunni's touch. I'm not sure why trust is such an important issue. I tell myself that she's just trying to make me feel welcome, but I'm getting that unsettling feeling in my stomach again, as if something is very wrong but I just don't know enough to see what it is yet.

"Here he comes," Sunni says.

I whip around, and Ethan's weaving his way through the bustling hallway. I wave and he waves back, smiling as he approaches us.

"Hey!" he says.

I hug my notebook closer to my chest. "Hey."

His eyes sweep over Sunni, Misty, Jia, and Wil, who are hovering around me. "You . . . still up for a tour?"

"Yes, definitely," I reply, maybe a little too quickly.

"I was going to stop by the greenhouse, so I'll tag along with you two, if y'all don't mind," Sunni says. "I have a key, so we could sneak a quick peek inside, if you want."

"Sure," Ethan says.

Oh. We aren't touring alone.

"Yeah, and I could get us into the tech building, up the road," Wil offers.

"The psych lab where I do work isn't that exciting," Jia says quietly, with a small smile. "We could always tour it later."

38

"Hey, I've got nothing else to do this afternoon. It's up to Ingrid what she wants to see." There's a sparkle in Ethan's eye, a kindness that reaches out and touches my stomach and twists it into knots. He doesn't seem upset that they want to join us, so I try not to let it bother me.

"Greenhouse, tech building—that all sounds good to me," I reply. "I saw some shops down the road, maybe we could check those out sometime too?"

"The tech building is near the bakery, and the café," Wil says.

Sunni's eyebrows rise. "We could get a bite to eat there."

I am feeling a little hungry, and I do have ten dollars cash on me. I think back to what my dad said about the meal plan, how expensive it is. *Maybe, just for today, I could go out, but I have to be careful not to make it a habit.*

Jia and Sunni quickly map out the most efficient route around campus that will hit all the highlights. Misty is playing with her phone, bored. *Why is she here if she doesn't want to come? Maybe she'll leave us alone.* She catches me staring. "What?" she spits.

"Nothing. I just . . . " I glance at her cell phone and reach for mine in my skirt pocket as I try to come up with an excuse. "I thought we didn't get great reception way out here."

She shrugs.

All right then.

Everyone else is stuffing their bags into the half-lockers. I stand awkwardly with Misty. She doesn't have a backpack or a notebook or anything. I shift the straps on my shoulder.

This laptop is going to be heavy to carry around campus.

Ethan steals a glance at me. "You can put your things in my locker for now, if you'd like."

My insides leap with joy. "Sure, thanks."

"I think there are a few lockers still available for rent," Sunni adds as she reattaches the lock on her locker. As it clicks shut, her grip tightens on it, and she lingers there,

39

as if caught up in another thought. Wil approaches her cautiously, but Sunni waves him away.

I wonder what that's about.

I give my things to Ethan and he carefully puts them in his locker. "I don't really use my locker much, since my paintings don't fit in here, so just let me know whenever you want to use it. The combo lock is ten, twenty-four, thirty-five."

"Thanks." My face feels hot.

We leave MacLeod Hall and head towards the greenhouse, since it's the closest. Sunni sticks close to me with Jia at her side. Wil walks ahead of us, hands in his pockets. He walks with his head down, because he's so tall, I guess. Misty trails behind, still fooling around with her phone.

Ethan is on my right. I try to think of something clever to say to him, but Sunni pipes up first. She fires off a million questions: Where am I from? What do I like to do in my spare time? I tell them about my musical accomplishments, and Sunni squeals in excitement.

"A musician! That's exactly what—!" She cuts herself off with a nervous laugh. "I mean . . . that's great."

I blush and steal a glance at Ethan. He's also beaming at me.

"I guess I could play for you sometime," I say.

Sunni looks away and nods, but the sadness is in her eyes again.

"You okay, Sunni?" Misty says from behind us.

"Yeah, fine," Sunni says, throwing Misty a wide grin that seems insincere.

"You sure?" I ask. "I mean, I don't have to play for you, I just thought . . . "

Sunni shakes her head. "No, no, it's not that. Just . . . don't mind me. Just . . . have a lot on my mind right now."

"About what Professor Jadore was talking about, your project on Joseph G. Campbell?"

Jia sucks in her breath and holds it, as if I've just

said a bad word. Sunni looks conflicted. "I shouldn't have mentioned that," she says quietly. "And neither should you."

"Why?" Ethan asks. "Joseph Campbell, as in *Hero with a Thousand Faces Joseph Campbell*? What's so bad about him?"

"Not that Joseph Campbell. Joseph G. Campbell," Sunni replies, her voice barely a whisper. "Just . . . I don't know. His name isn't that respected in academic circles, by those who actually know his name. It's probably better y'all don't say anythin' about him in tutorial or anywhere else. All right?"

"Okay," I say. I make a mental note to look him up later when I'm alone.

Ethan shrugs and reaches into his pocket. "I spend most of my time in a studio alone, so I won't say his name to anyone. Anyone want some gum?"

"I'll have some," Misty says. She speeds her walk and catches up with the rest of us, holding out her palm.

"Didn't the doctor tell you not to chew gum with your tongue piercing?" Jia asks. She looks uncomfortable.

Misty shrugs. "I'm not letting anyone tell me what to do with my body."

Ethan punches out a piece into Misty's hand and turns to me. "Gum?"

Usually I'm not a big gum person, but since Ethan is offering . . .

"Sure."

He pulls out the plastic holder for the gum, revealing two pieces left in the pack. "Aw. Here, just take it. I've got tons back in the room."

"Oh, thanks," I say, pocketing the pack and mentally inscribing likes gum onto the list I'm compiling about him. So far *hot British accent* and *re-watch all David Tennant* Doctor Who *episodes to fawn over likeness* are the top two entries.

We're almost to the greenhouse. It's across the road from the cluster of residences, right on the roundabout, near the main street that would take us into Sparkstone's shopping district and private suburbs. The entire building is see-through. Cultivated greenery twists its way to the top of the structure. Behind the building is a group of maple trees, which acts as a privacy barrier between the main road and the goings-on inside the sheer greenhouse. I see two people inside, watering plants and making observations on a clipboard. I wonder how they install the blood-taking door system on a building made of wood and thick, transparent tarps.

Sunni digs out a white swipe card from her pocket. On the door, I see a mechanical black box with a pinprick of red light shining on the side.

So there is some sort of digital system to let people in and out. I know it's in the school's best interest to keep everything secure, but who's going to steal stuff from a greenhouse? *This is a little ridiculous.*

"We won't stay in here long," Sunni promises. "I don't wanna interrupt the others."

"What sort of plants do you grow here?" I ask.

"Oh, a bit of everything!" Sunni's eyes light up as she launches into an explanation of every flower, every vegetable, every bit of greenery that she's studied and grown. Misty, who had been texting, puts her phone away and gives Sunni her undivided attention. I'm also listening, until something odd catches my attention.

Behind the greenhouse, in the array of maple trees, someone is kneeling over a large, black ventilation system. At least, I think it's a ventilation system. It seems odd, though, to have such a thing on a greenhouse. The man—dressed in a guard's one-piece, navy-blue overalls uniform and an orange construction vest—tinkers with the mechanical system. He hums a tune that ascends the scale in the key of A major, switches briefly to C minor, and descends the scale again in A major. The tune starts slow, in two-four time, and then speeds up to the point where all the notes seem to be hummed at once, and then just as abruptly, he slows the melody again.

I veer away from the group and peer around the greenhouse. I don't want to get too close and disturb his work, but the tune has piqued my curiosity. He happens to lift his head and wipe sweat off his brow, and that's when I recognize his face.

It's the guard from the gate.

This isn't suspicious, I tell myself as I back away slowly. *The guy probably has lots of jobs around the campus.*

But then I see it's not a hand holding his wrench. It's a tentacle.

I barely suffocate a scream.

"Hey, Ingrid! What are you looking at?" Ethan asks.

The rest of the group hurries towards me, except Wil. He's stopped, one hand resting on his temple.

My scream wasn't quiet enough. A snarl twists the guard's face. The tentacle drops the wrench as it slithers back up his sleeve.

"What is that guy?" I ask.

I get no answer from my newfound friends. Ethan looks puzzled. Wil moves in slow motion towards us, concentrating on something else. And Jia . . . *Where is Jia? She was just here a second ago.*

I take my gaze off the man for one second. Just one. When I look back, he's barrelling towards us. Towards *me*. The hatred in his gaze is so fierce I stumble backwards—into Sunni.

"GET DOWN!" she screams, and shoves me out of the way.

I hit the walkway with a thud. My head spins and the ground rumbles. What sounds like a lion's roar echoes throughout the campus. I start to get up but Sunni holds me down and covers my eyes.

"Hey! What are you—?"

"Don't look," she whispers in my ear. "Please. Just don't."

"Why? I need to see. What's going on?"

I wrestle with Sunni's grip but she's stronger than she looks. The roar comes again, but this time, screams follow. Sounds of explosions and something gurgling and claws ripping through clothing—*is someone being ripped apart?*

Misty yells something but no one responds, and I smell grass burning. I have to do something.

There's a cell phone in my pocket.

Even this far out on the prairies 911 must work.

"Just . . . let . . . me . . . " I throw Sunni's hand off my eyes.

Fire burns the lawn and creeps dangerously close to the greenhouse. The two people who'd been working there before are gone. The guard is also gone: in his place is a five-foot-tall lump of beige and red flesh and a large, screaming mouth with circular rows of small, dark teeth. Hundreds of tentacles writhe and squirm in the air. And Misty, she's running towards the monster, yelling profanities, running *into* the fiery wall that surrounds the creature.

No. That's not right. The fire, it's coming *from* Misty. Her hands are shooting fire and ice, coating the greenhouse in icicles and patches of ever-burning flame.

"Is this . . . real?" I ask.

Within arm's reach, Ethan is out cold, cuts and scrapes marring his freckled face. I have to make sure he's okay. Trying to shake Sunni, I feel a sharp stabbing pain boring into my temples, and Wil is running for me, hands outstretched, and then . . . darkness.

CHAPTER 4

I don't know where I am.

The scent of fresh flowers drifts in and out of my nostrils, so I must be outside. My head rests on the most comfortable ball of fluff and my body feels warm. Secure. I smile but my face hurts.

Slowly, things come into focus as my brain wakes up and starts asking questions. I'm lying in bed, and there's a door across from me. Same layout as my temporary room at Sparkstone. *Ugh. Still at Sparkstone.* But it's not my room. Potted flowers sit to my right: large daffodils. They reach to the sun and beg to be warm.

Curled up in a large red armchair to my left is Sunni. Her hair is frizzier than it was this morning and the dark circles beneath her eyelids seem more pronounced. She holds no book, no electronic devices—nothing to pass the time. She stares at me while my vision clears, her eyes the epitome of hope and worry.

"You're okay," she says, sitting up in the armchair.

"Where . . . ?" My voice is croaky, as if I haven't spoken in a million years.

"My room," she replies. Embarrassment shows through her freckled cheeks. "We didn't take you to the infirmary. You just have a couple of scrapes and bruises, from your . . . fall." The last word is uncertain. Practiced.

I sit up. The left side of my face hurts from the tiny rocks that had dug into it. I rub my cheek tenderly. Sunni's room is a personification of the cheery side of her personality. Large bay windows let in light from the setting sun behind us. Reds and yellows are cast on the painted bright-blue walls. The bed faces the door, and there's a large bathroom right across from me. The floor is a dark hardwood that's so clean it acts as a mirror for the sunlight. To my left, behind Sunni, there's a fish tank filled with goldfish that casts yet another light show on the floor. I feel as if I'm in a five-star hotel in a large city rather than middle-of-nowhere Alberta.

And my room can look just as posh, when the designers are done with it.

Anything to make the students comfortable, Ms. Agailya had said.

I'm so taken aback by the scenery that I forget why I'm tucked in Sunni's bed in the first place. My mind rattles as it pieces together the events leading up to me waking up here.

"You . . . you held me down," I say.

Sunni's expression is pained, and it makes her look so much older than her seventeen years. "You . . . you hit your head pretty hard . . . "

"I don't think that's what happened." I'm sure of this, even though I don't remember everything exactly. "There was some kind of monster . . . and fire burning everywhere, and icicles that wouldn't melt, and a *roar* . . . " I cover my ears because the sound is still echoing in my mind. "It was *so* real. I *saw* things . . . things that can't be real, things that I see on TV and read about in stories, but they looked too real to be fake. Did you see . . . ?"

I trail off because Sunni doesn't appear to be listening. Her eyes are far away.

Peeling off the blankets, I slide to the edge of the bed. My boots are sitting neatly by the door, but otherwise, I'm still wearing the same clothes as this morning. I sit so that our knees are almost touching.

"What happened to me?" I ask.

Her voice is low and she talks with her head down. "It's not about what's happenin' to you. It's about what we have. We have to protect each other."

"Protect each other from what? What do we have? Why are we whispering?"

Sunni juts her chin to the upper right corner above the door, and I see it. A tiny camera is embedded into the wall. Its red light is a laser that keeps a watchful eye on the two of us.

"I only noticed it after I brought ya here," she whispers, shading her mouth with her hand. "I'm sorry. If I had known they were watchin' me . . . I shoulda known . . . "

I nod, casting a suspicious glance at the camera, because I don't know what else to do. *Is this even legal? I don't think so.* I wonder who would want to spy on Sunni, who seemed so innocent, and why they would find her so fascinating. *If Sunni is being watched, does that mean there's a camera hidden somewhere in my temporary room? What if they are not only busy making my regular room look amazing, but also installing high-tech spy cameras everywhere?*

So many questions, too few answers.

And then I suddenly remember.

"Ethan." His name tingles on my tongue. I remember the bruises on his face. "Is he okay?"

"Wil looked after him," Sunni says. She looks somewhat relieved that I've changed of subject. "I think he took him to the infirmary. His injuries were a little more serious. But not that much more serious."

"Oh." I wonder if I should go visit him to make sure he's okay, and if he's as worried about me as I am about him. I wonder if he even thinks of me at all, or if I'm just some girl he met today.

"You have any brothers or sisters, Ingrid?"

I'm not sure why she's asking me this. Maybe it's to distract us from the camera. I shake my head. "Just me and my parents."

She nods. "Just been me and my mama, too. Daddy was in the navy, always out at sea for some reason for long trips and missions, but then he just never came home one day." She shrugs it off as if she's told the story a thousand times to a thousand different people, but there's a heaviness in her eyes, as though somehow this retelling of the tale is important. "Mama took it real hard, even though lookin' back on it, maybe she knew he wasn't comin' home. She always hoped, though. She would always be sittin' in that chair upstairs in her room, and it overlooked the little pond in our backyard. Maybe she was pretendin' he was just a hop, skip, and a jump away, that that little pond was the big, blue ocean, and that someday, someday . . . well." She tries to shrug again but the nonchalance just isn't in her. "Sendin' me here, it was hard for her. She'd say, 'Sunniva, don't you dare go away and leave me here all by my lonesome.' I think she was afraid that like my daddy, I'd never come home again."

A silence descends between the two of us as I search for something appropriate to say. She gives me a half-grin. "I'm blabberin' away. I don't blame you for thinkin' I'm crazy, really." She steals a glance at the camera again. "I just . . . I just think that there might be a time when I'm not gonna go home. And then Mama really will be alone." Reaching out, she squeezes my left hand. "Don't you let them make you think that you're alone. 'Cause you're not, y'hear?"

My mouth is dry. "Okay."

"Don't let them scare you. Don't show them that you're scared. I've . . . I've seen things . . . " She's whispering now. "And I know how some of it's going to play out. Just . . . just promise me, whatever happens . . . " Tears line her eyes.

I frown. "Promise what? Sunni, why are you crying?"

She leans even closer to my ear. "I can see things . . . that haven't happened yet. In my dreams." Her voice is a trembling whisper.

There's a black *thud* in my stomach. "That's how you knew I was coming."

"Yes."

"What . . . what else did you see about me?"

Hidden sorrow and the stories that accompany it threatens to spill from her eyes. "Some of it I don't understand. But you're not here by accident. They want you here. And so do we. You can *help* us. But listen carefully. You can't help *me*. I am already lost. Do y'hear?"

I sit in stunned silence. My heart is drumming up a storm and there's a high-pitched ringing in my ears. "Sunni, why can't I help you?"

She pulls her hand away from mine and gets up from the armchair. "Knowin' everyone's secrets, it's a terrible burden. If they get a hold of me, it's all over. So don't think about me. I know you'll do the right thing. Make the right choice, and all." Sniffling, she wipes her tears away with the back of her hand. "I'm just gonna go pee. You'll be all right here?"

"Uh, yeah," I say.

She disappears into the bathroom and shuts the door, and I take a moment to process everything Sunni has just said. *Don't let them scare you. Promise me . . .* Promise her what? That I won't tell anyone about Misty shooting fire and ice from her bare hands? Who would believe me, anyway?

My parents might. Maybe Ethan, too.

The camera evaluates my dishevelled appearance. I slip my bare legs back under the covers because they feel naked without my boots. Propping up the pillow on the baseboard, my hand slips under the second pillow beside me and brushes against something hard. Lifting the pillow, I sneak a peek. It's a journal. The cover is nothing special: just paper-bag brown, something you might buy at the dollar store. There's no title on the front, no warnings saying *Keep out: Sunni's diary.* Tiny scrapes are embedded into the front and back, and the edges are frayed and bent from constant use.

I know I shouldn't open it. It's probably personal. I wouldn't want Sunni opening my harp and strumming her fingers across its beautiful strings or touching my keyboard without my permission.

No. I should put it back.

But Sunni is still in the bathroom.

My fingers wrap around the edge of the binding. I open the journal, just a crack, enough to let the red sunlight shine through onto its pages. I can see some sprawling, frantic cursive. And some pictures? I open it a little wider. Yes, definitely pictures, quick sketches of people and things interspersed with shorthand, messy writing.

Well, the book is already half open. There's no turning back now. I spread it flat on my lap and flip through the pages. No sign of white space anywhere. Every inch of every page is used, covered in illegible scribbles and hasty sketches. I flip the pages as quietly as possible. Reading the entries would be too personal, I decide, but different sentences jump out at me: *Round, fiery circle dances in the darkness. Step quickly, step through! Wind through the thicket, breathe it in, until you are its master.*

In the middle of the journal, a giant double helix twists and turns across the fold, taking up both pages. It looks carefully drawn. It must be important. In neat cursive, Sunni has written: *Gene 213. What binds us all together.*

I turn more pages. Every few paragraphs there's a date, and the deeper I go into the book, the more recent the entries become. I find myself reading; I can't help myself. The writing isn't meant to be skimmed. It's too poetic. Amidst the conspiracy surrounding the school, all of this beauty is swirling around in Sunni's head, waiting to be expressed.

I tear myself away from the words to flip a few more pages and then pause at a full-page sketch of a man's face. It's not as detailed as the double helix. In fact, it's one of the more hurried sketches in the collection. Thick eyebrows, intense gaze, pointed nose and chin. Scribbled traces of hair suggest it's flying in the wind, as if he's constantly moving. I want to turn the page but his eyes, as rough as they are drawn, freeze me in place.

Somehow, I *know* this man is someone important, someone I am supposed to know but can't name because everything about him is out of reach. Beneath the portrait are three initials: *J.G.C.* Could this be the man Sunni was talking about during tutorial? Joseph G. Campbell?

The camera is watching, I remember suddenly.

The toilet flushes and water gushes into the bathroom sink. I quickly stuff the journal beneath the pillow, being careful to leave it exactly as I found it, as Sunni opens the door.

My mind scrambles for a camera-appropriate topic to distract Sunni with if necessary when a flurry of voices in the hallway draws her attention. The voices become louder as they near the door. It bursts open. The doorknob slams into the wall, and Misty stands in the doorway as if she's storming into her domain and not Sunni's. Jia and Wil are behind her, peering over Misty's shoulder at me with a shared concern.

Though Misty's entrance is formidable and a little intimidating, Sunni is right there in her face, blocking the way. "Y'all shouldn't be in here." She points above the door, a quick gesture that I almost miss.

"When was that . . . ?" Misty trails off and twists her lips. She surveys the rumpled blankets on Sunni's bed and how my legs are intertwined with them. Her poisonous stare burns into my face, heating my cheeks. "Tell her to get out of your room, Sunni."

"I'm not tellin' her anything like that. She's hurt. Or, she was. She looks better now." She says the last part louder, to the camera.

I throw the blankets aside and stand up, straightening out my skirt. My head pounds as if a thousand people are knocking on my skull. I smile and pretend to be well for the camera's sake. For Sunni's sake.

Misty chews on her thumb and its chipped-off black nail polish. "She doesn't look that roughed up."

"Ethan was worse," Jia says, earning a *stop talking* look from both Sunni and Misty.

"Have you seen him?" I ask, a little too quickly.

The girls look to Wil. He clears his throat. His voice is hoarse, as if he's not used to talking. "I heard he was released from the infirmary a few hours ago."

"I should . . . make sure he's all right." It feels lame to say. I don't even know him.

"Yeah. We should get out of here," Misty says, backing away from the door.

I don't blame her. I don't like the camera watching me either.

Don't look at the camera. Don't look.

I take deliberate steps to the door, where my boots are standing at attention and waiting for my feet to be one with them again. I feel everyone watching me.

I hope they don't come with me to find Ethan.

Trouble seems to like these four, and if there are cameras watching me everywhere I go, I want to stay out of the limelight.

"It's after five," Sunni says. "Ingrid, did you want to come down to the Evergreen Café with us? I'll buy you dinner."

"Uh, no thanks," I say, shoving my right foot into my boot.

Sunni tries again. "The food is no good here." Desperation coats her voice. "I know ya had a crappy afternoon, but let me try to make it up to ya."

"I think I'll take my chances with the cafeteria food, thanks."

Sunni starts to speak again but Misty sneers. "Don't take it personally. She's just after the hipster Brit."

My face flushes as I stomp my left foot into my boot. "No." But my objection is weak, and Wil is smirking at me.

"This isn't funny. She could . . . " Sunni trails off. "Ingrid, please. Don't eat. If you do—"

"What?" I interject. "Tell me, or don't tell me. Don't give me half-answers."

The camera whirs above us as it moves, tilting so that I am at the centre of its focus.

Sunni stares at me with such raw emotion that my stomach feels as though it's being ripped open, as if my outburst hurt her more than I could imagine. *Could the food really be that bad?* It is such a small request, that I eat with them at the café down the road. *I can always find Ethan later. He never tried to find me.*

But before I can give in, Misty takes me by the arm and drags me into the hallway. I stumble because I'm just getting used to my boots again. With a strength that surprises me, she slams me against the wall and stands at the entrance to Sunni's room like an overprotective troll.

"Speak to her like that again," Misty warns, "and you will never *deserve* answers."

The word twists my pride. *Deserve* answers? My entire life I'd worked hard to *deserve* good things: A+ in every class, top marks in any competition involving English or science, and near-the-top-of-the-class status in mathematics. I'd never felt *undeserving* of something. It's a strange feeling, and I want to shout, *No, I deserve to know this mystery. Tell me what you know about the world that I don't.*

"We can meet her after she eats in the cafeteria," Sunni says quietly. "In the greenhouse. It's been cleaned up, and no one is scheduled to work on their projects there tonight. You'll get your . . . answers."

"I can come get you," Jia offers.

"I can find it," I say, because I want to show them that I am self-reliant, and more importantly, because I don't know if I will be at Sparkstone after supper.

One clunky step backwards, and then another, and then I'm walking steadily down the corridor. Sunni's bedroom door shuts behind me. I keep my face expressionless as my eyes rapidly scan the corridor for cameras. There's one—no, two! One above the entrance to the floor, by the elevators and the stairs, and another halfway down the hallway. It's pointed at Sunni's room, but it follows me as I walk.

I take the stairs and count three more cameras. They're not well hidden, but most are stuck onto the high ceilings, and I doubt many students would crane their necks up that often. I wonder how many cameras I'm *not* counting.

There's a small landing on the stairs, with a secured door to another floor. Two men on ladders are fixing an electrical panel above me and they give me strange looks. They're wearing the same navy overalls and orange construction vests as the guard at the gate. One of them is tapping a small key pad on the side of a black, beeping box. I avert my gaze and concentrate on not tripping as I continue my descent.

My heeled boots dig into the soft grass outside Rita House. I look both ways before crossing the deserted road to Rogers Hall. I wonder if anyone else saw the man with the tentacle arm, or the fire that came from nowhere. Pulling my sleeve over my hand as I open the door to Rogers Hall, I look up, and sure enough, a security camera is staring right at me. Inside, I count one camera above the reception desk. There is another in the hallway, but it's at the end, not in the middle, and it doesn't appear to be on. Until I look at it.

I run the rest of the way to my bedroom and unlock the door. I hurry inside and shut the door cautiously. Turning on the light, I inspect the upper corners. No cameras. Maybe I'm not interesting enough after all. I even check the bathroom and feel relieved when my search comes up empty.

Someone else has been in my room, however. On the bed is a white plastic card with a sticky note attached. It reads:

Ingrid, this is your temporary key card. Use it to access the cafeteria, the gym, and most other places on campus. Come talk to me tomorrow. — Grace Agailya.

I crumple up the sticky note, pocket the key card, and chance a look up. My heart drops into my stomach. It looks like a chopped black olive is stuck to the ceiling. After unzipping my boots, I discard them at the foot of the bed and climb on top of the mattress. It's such a small thing, this black circle, and hard like plastic. I squint. It looks like there's something reflective in the middle of the hole. *No, please no . . .*

My fingernail can barely fit inside. When I tap it, it feels like glass.

A camera.

No, no, no. No one is going to watch me sleep. No one is going to invade my privacy, no one.

Digging into the sewn-on pocket of my skirt, I pull out the gum Ethan gave me earlier. I pop the last piece into my mouth, chew for a few minutes, and allow the minty freshness to overwhelm my senses. When the burst of flavour is gone, I pull out the chewed piece and smear it over the camera lens.

There. Have that, why don't you.

I think about the gum falling on me when I'm sleeping and it getting caught in my hair. But I'd rather deal with gum in my hair than be watched at night by someone . . . or some*thing*.

I spend the next fifteen minutes thoroughly searching the ceiling for more olive-shaped cameras, but there seems to be only one. Putting my boots back on, I make two promises to myself.

First promise: I will meet with Sunni and her friends and find out what really happened this afternoon. There's definitely something out-of-this-world happening with them, but at least Sunni had the decency to tell me about the cameras and took care of me while I was unconscious, so they can't be out to harm me.

The second promise I make for my own safety: No matter what, I will find a way to get out of Sparkstone.

CHAPTER 5

It's as if the veil has been pulled from my eyes and I'm seeing the school for the first time.

Crowds of students, well dressed and well groomed and well educated, head for the cafeteria. Two cameras whir above the entrance, silently scanning each student as the young minds swipe their key cards on the machine. A woman sits behind the tall black card scanner, staring at a computer monitor. Each time a card is swiped, the woman's computer beeps and the student continues through the cafeteria doors. I take the key card from my pocket and press it against the tall black scan machine.

A longer beep. People in line behind me sigh and scoff in frustration.

"Oh, Ingrid Stanley," the woman at the desk says. She looks over her glasses at the monitor and then smiles thinly at me. "You missed lunch today."

"Yeah, I . . . " It occurs to me that I can't provide a solid explanation as to where I was. "I guess I did miss it. Sorry."

"Not a problem," the woman replies. "We just like to regulate things, so we can keep our food supply consistent. Expensive to ship this far north sometimes."

It's not that far north. It would be way more expensive to ship to somewhere like Nunavut, I want to say, but I don't want to make trouble.

"If you plan on skipping a meal again, just let reception know," she continues.

"Come on, hurry UP!" someone in line shouts.

"Uh sure," I say quickly. "Can I go now?"

"Enjoy your meal," she says, and gestures me forward.

I throw open the door. Rows upon rows of long tables line what looks like an antique banquet hall, and the air is filled with wonderful smells: chicken, baked tomatoes, brownies, spicy curries—all different things that normally wouldn't seem appealing together, but my mouth is watering like crazy. I don't recall being this hungry before stepping into the cafeteria, but now I want to murder everyone in line just so I can grab a fat, juicy steak and devour it in one bite.

About fifty students are in front of me. I grab a freshly washed tray and some utensils from the stack to my right. The line disappears around a partition, where a cafeteria worker serves hot food from behind a counter. Behind her is a busy industrial kitchen, teeming with line cooks, chefs, and dishwashers. All the workers wear pristine white chef jackets and chef hats. They smile as they scoop all manner of foods onto porcelain plates. Some students grab the food right from the workers' hands, slam it on the tray, and race for the next food station. In fact, most of the students in front of me share that nervous dance of anticipation: especially the obese students.

Maybe Sunni's right. I need to get out of here.

But the line moves quickly, and the closer I get to the hot food, the more I want it. There are labeled sections on the assembly line, and the first one I get to is the soup section. Tomato-basil is the special today. I don't know if I've ever tried tomato-basil soup in my life, but when the smell wafts into my nose, I know it's exactly what I want.

"I'll take a bowl of that," I say to the cafeteria worker as I point at the rich red soup pooled in a pot sunk into the stainless steel counter.

"Certainly," the worker replies, and scoops a ladleful into a deep bowl.

"More," I find myself saying.

Her smile widens to a grin. She scoops more into the bowl. Nothing spills or goes flying: she's done this a thousand times. Her teeth are bleached white, just like her chef jacket, and they're as straight as the rows of tables behind me. "You'll love this. We made it special today."

There's something wrong with her statement, but I smile anyway. My mouth is full of drool. "That's great. Thank you."

The bowl is comfortably warm as I lift it from the counter and place it on my tray. I grab a bun from a basket next to the soup lady. Although other delicious treats and meals call to me, there's nothing else I want than to find a seat. I have to eat this soup, right now! Almost every place is taken. *I probably should've just come straight to the cafeteria from Sunni's room, to beat the rush.*

I'm about to give up and drink the soup while standing when I spot him. In hundreds of students, I can pick him out, and for a split second, I don't care about tomato-basil soup.

"Ethan!" I call. My voice is lost in the sound of hundreds of people slurping and chewing and talking about interesting facts they learned today. I speed as quickly as I can without spilling the soup, weaving my way through the rows, until I reach him. He's reading something on his phone. The person sitting across from him gets up and takes his dirty dishes and tray; I quickly claim the spot.

He looks up immediately as I settle in the chair. "Ingrid!"

My stomach feels fuzzy and warm when I hear him say my name in his thick British accent. "Hi," I say, more shyly now.

"I was wondering where you went. They told me at the infirmary that you never checked in, so I just assumed you were all right. You are all right, aren't you?" His gaze is intense as his eyes dance all over my face, inspecting every pore.

"I'm fine. I just . . . I went to sleep for a few hours," I say. "But you? You're all right? I saw you fall hard on the pavement . . . "

There's a bandage hiding behind his bangs. He rubs it tenderly. "Oh no, I'm fine. Just a bump."

I was worried about you, I want to say, but it seems too intimate to admit.

He smiles and starts eating again—a turkey sandwich with a side of fries—and my intense hunger returns. I reach for my spoon. Sunni's warning floats through my mind but the wafting aroma of the tomato-basil soup invades my nostrils and teases me with the promise of the most satisfying meal in the world. The spoon fills with the red, creamy liquid, and like a dream, time skips ahead and my lips are wrapped around the spoon. Flavour explodes in my mouth. So delicious. Beyond delicious. Heavenly. My stomach growls for more. I can't get this soup in my stomach fast enough.

"All right there, Ingrid?" Ethan asks.

His voice makes me pause. My soup bowl is half empty and I feel remnants of basil on the corners of my lips. *Did I just wolf that down in front of him?*

"This soup is really good. They must have the most awesome chefs in the world if the food is this good," I say, grabbing a napkin and dabbing my lips.

"Yeah, all the food here is great," he replies. "But I don't think they have a culinary program. Just . . . brilliant chefs."

"I guess . . . I guess I was expecting poorer quality food."

Sunni's warning returns. But while she was showing me the cameras, she was being overly paranoid. So she was probably exaggerating about the food too. Or maybe she's vegetarian, or a vegan, or she can't eat Sparkstone's food for allergy reasons. Looking around, I see that everyone has licked their plates clean. So nothing's wrong with the food, other than that most people can't get enough of it.

"Sparkstone doesn't settle for anything less than perfect," Ethan says, putting a hand on his stomach. He's not like the obese guys in line. I wonder what lies beneath his shirt and if his muscles are toned.

It takes a lot of strength, but I push the tray away. Thinking about Ethan—talking to Ethan—seems to keep the uncontrollable hunger at bay. "If I ask you something, would you answer me straight? Tell me the truth?"

Ethan sets down his sandwich and looks serious. "Yeah, 'course. Something wrong?"

"I . . . don't know," I admit slowly. I push the tray even further away so that I can lean forward without the soup's intoxicating, delicious smell taking over my senses. "Did you . . . I don't know . . . see anything strange before you blacked out?"

He frowns and looks more confused. "What do you mean, strange?"

"Like . . . fire. Explosions . . . " *A fleshy tentacle monster*, I want to say, but it's too strange to say aloud.

"No, I didn't see anything like that. Why, you saw something like that?"

There's genuine concern on his face. Tension I didn't know I had dispenses into the air as I exhale. "Well . . . maybe." I tear the freshly baked bun into bits, letting the pieces fall in my soup. "Sunni said I fell pretty hard, hit my head. So I don't know, maybe I'm crazy."

"Fell? I thought I saw her push you."

So maybe I'm not crazy. "Yeah?"

"Before I got knocked down, it looked like Sunni tackled you. Like something big was coming and she was trying to get you out of the way. Took you down pretty fast, too."

"What took you out?"

"Me?" He laughs. His eye tooth is crooked and I love it. "Something from behind. Barely felt a thing. I think Wil or someone must've accidently knocked me over in the commotion. Which would be fine if . . . " He trails off a bit, studies my face, and looks mildly uncomfortable.

"If what?" I prompt.

He shakes his head. "Well . . . I don't know. Head's a bit fuzzy I guess. I'm having trouble remembering things. I wish I could remember what happened more clearly, but we were just going to the greenhouse to look at Sunni's plants, right? And then . . . and then I guess I fell and hit my head . . . " He looks concerned again. "I'm sorry, Ingrid. But I think I've always had trouble remembering things." He frowns, as if he's not sure that what he's saying is completely true. "My parents say I'm too caught up in my art to pay attention to what's happening in the real world."

I frown. "Well . . . I hope you don't suddenly forget me," I say before I can stop myself.

He blushes. "No, 'course not. People I'm fine with, it's mostly just stuff from a long time ago. Ever since I came to Canada, I've been having a hard time remembering the streets surrounding the place where I grew up, the kids I played with. Stuff like that."

My heart breaks for him. I can't even imagine not being able to recall things from my childhood.

"Coming from England to Canada is a big life change. A lot to take in. Probably enough to make you forget a few things. It'll come back to you though, I hope," I reply.

"Yeah, I suppose. Anyway, maybe it's just the bump on my head that's causing the trouble now, and mixing me up. Nasty though, isn't it?" He points to the bandage again. "Thank God I don't have any self-portraits to do in the next little while. Speaking of which, had a favour I wanted to ask you. If you were up for it."

"Oh. Sure, what is it?" Butterflies flap frantic wings in my stomach.

"Well, for one of the projects I'm working on, I have to do a series of character studies, and use real models. And well . . . I just thought you had the right look, is all." He twirls a fry between his forefinger and his thumb.

So much for the plan to leave Sparkstone.

"You don't have to be nude," he adds quickly. "But um . . . if you have anything tight fitting . . . that would be helpful. And you can wear those boots. They're fantastic."

"They're my favourite," I admit.

"And you look smashing in them. So . . . is that a yes then? Would you be able to come over tonight? I mean. Wow, I guess that's pretty forward of me, isn't it?" His cheeks flush pink. "Can't risk Ms. Agailya getting mad at me again, even though she's the tamest out of the profs. There's an art studio in this building, on the third floor. Public, other students use it too. And like I said, you don't have to be naked or anything, so . . . so that's a plus."

"That's the second time you said I don't *have* to be naked."

"Yeah . . . well . . . I dunno." He runs a hand through his floppy hair. "I just want to make sure you're comfortable and all."

"I would love to be a model for you," I say, grinning so hard it hurts. "But I . . . I kind of promised Sunni and them that I'd hang out with them tonight. But maybe afterwards I can come by, if that's not too late?"

"No, that's brilliant. I do my best work when it's dark anyway." He grins again and I melt a little bit.

And maybe after that, I can escape. Maybe.

"Sounds good."

"Let me put your number in my phone, just in case you get lost on the way to the building." He produces his phone again and taps his thumbs on the screen while I dictate my number, my heart leaping just a little bit with each digit.

He can call me whenever he wants. Whenever he wants!

"I don't suppose this is entirely fair, you knowing my number, me not knowing yours."

Tap, tap, tap. Ethan grins, and then, my phone vibrates. I draw it out of my skirt pocket. One new text message:

Your beauty is unfair to the world.

"I'll see you tonight, yeah?" He gets up from the table, carrying his tray of half-finished food.

My body is ready to explode with words, comebacks, and flirtations, but all I can do is nod and grin like a fool.

He deposits his tray on some racks at the other end of the cafeteria, grabs an apple from a basket near the exit, and tosses it from palm to palm as he leaves. I sit there for five minutes at least, thinking things I shouldn't about a guy I just met.

The tantalizing smell of my soup calls to my stomach as I pick up my tray and head for the racks. I'm still a bit hungry but I resist the urge to eat anything else. My stomach is a mix of euphoria and anticipation. If I weren't wearing my boots and if there weren't cameras watching my every move, I'd skip out of the cafeteria and spread my joy to as many people as possible. I haven't even been here one day, and already I have a crush on a guy. Feels longer than a day, being here, what with being unconscious and the fiery-icy magic and creature-thing attacking.

Thinking about the tentacle monster is sobering. I have to get out of this cafeteria and head to the greenhouse to see Sunni, and then meet up with Ethan . . . and then . . . and then . . .

Escape. Maybe Ethan will come with me if I ask him.

It's a dumb thought. The whole idea of escaping is really far-fetched. The woman at the entrance to the cafeteria eyes me with suspicion as I leave. Above me, the camera whirs as it follows me down the hallway, towards reception. Where would I even go if I escaped? Sparkstone, the town, is gated. Around us is nothing but the Canadian prairies, small farms and abandoned towns, clumps of trees, and highway. Even if I had a car, it would be a long drive back to Calgary, to my parents.

But Ethan. Ethan . . .

His name gives me strength. Speaking it will unlock any door, solve any problem.

My face heats, and I'm smiling like an idiot again.

There's a set of stairs before me leading up to the front entrance. It would be so easy to just run outside, through the town and up to the gate. Away from the cameras, away from my new peers who have more secrets than I feel comfortable knowing in a lifetime. Away from the cute Brit who intoxicates my mind.

My euphoria mixes with a new feeling, something toxic that seeps through my stomach and spreads its infection through my veins—and up my oesophagus.

Oh God. I'm going to throw up.

There's a trash can immediately up the stairs, next to the unattended security desk. I dash towards it and spew the soup I just ate and part of the bacon-and-egg breakfast I ate this morning.

Sunni was right. There's something about the food that does not agree with me. Something . . . toxic.

I stealthily wipe my mouth on my sleeve and glance around to see if anyone caught my embarrassing moment. Several girls coming up the stairs give me strange looks and one asks if I'm all right, but I wave her away and say I'm fine. Hopefully whatever was in the food that made me crazy earlier is flushed out of my system.

As I hurry up the adjacent stars and down the corridor to my room, I pull out my cell phone. Dialling my parents and telling them that the school is trying to poison me sounds stupid. Telling them that I've made a mistake in coming here sounds even stupider. It would mean admitting that I'm too afraid to compete with people who might be smarter than me. I input the number and stare at it for a few seconds before deleting it again. I have to be strong. I can figure this out. I am not stupid.

I have to be brave.

The hallway lights are a gross yellow and all the doors on the floor are closed. *Is there even anyone else on this floor?* Ms. Agailya said there are only temporary rooms on this floor. But the lights are dark under the doors. Just me, alone on a floor with seventeen other bedrooms the size of luxury hotel suites. My boots clunk on the ratty carpet and disturb the unnatural silence.

Three feet from my dorm, I halt.

My bedroom door is ajar.

I stare at the sliver of yellow light invading my bedroom. *I closed and locked the door when I left . . . right?* The key is heavy in my pocket. *Yes, I definitely locked it.* Maybe someone from reception was looking for me while I was in Sunni's room, for some non-creepy reason regarding registration. After all, Ms. Agailya had entered earlier to leave my key card.

Or maybe . . .

The creature, and the fire and the ice erupting from Misty's fingertips . . .

Down the hallway, it is still quiet. My heart quickens, pounding in my ears. There is still a chance to escape. To find Sunni and the others, to call Ethan or my parents, to go anywhere else but inside my dorm.

It's still quiet as I step towards the door. What kind of person would I be if I ran away from potential danger? The Doctor would never shy away. Neither would Captain Kirk or Captain Picard. They'd throw open the door and deal with whatever was inside, peacefully. Words are their weapons.

I have words. And I have my steel-toed boots. That will have to be enough.

I nudge the door with the toe of my boot. It creaks open, letting more hallway light in. Drawing in a deep breath, I punch the light switch on. I blink. And I blink again.

No one is in the room.

I breathe a sigh of relief. *Working myself up, all for nothing!* A laugh escapes from deep within my stomach and fills the air with a joyous noise that makes me feel not so alone anymore. I'm so *dumb!* Cameras or no cameras, I am getting way too paranoid. Too many TV shows about aliens.

I throw the door shut.

A deep growl joins my laughter.

I don't think I'm alone anymore.

The air shimmers before my bed and a massive blob that looks like lumpy tofu blinks into existence. Tentacles, rounded off with knobby flesh, writhe from the fleshy blob in every direction. But the mouth . . . that's the most terrifying part of all. The entire front part of its body is a mouth with three sets of small sharp teeth, spiralling down into its throat. Droplets of saliva fall onto the carpet as it opens its mouth wider and draws a raspy breath. It slithers closer. The smell of an unwashed body hovers around the creature. It's not pungent, but it makes me feel icky all the same.

I can't be completely certain, but I think this is the thing I saw earlier, by the greenhouse, before I blacked out.

I clutch the V-neck of my shirt in fear, and gather my wits. "What are you?"

"Mistress said for me to keep watch on you," it replies.

It has no eyes, so I wonder how it can keep watch on anything at all. A broom lies against the wall, beside the door. I grab it and it becomes my weapon. "Stay back."

The creature spits as it opens its mouth wider. A sound erupts from its gut: it's laughing. "I will not hurt the Crosskey."

"The what?"

Obviously English can't be its first language. But . . . Crosskey? What could that mean if it isn't messing up its words?

"If you don't leave this room . . . or this planet . . . right now, I'll stab you with my very powerful, very *sharp* weapon."

I hold out the blunt end of the broom.

It laughs again. "Your stick can't hurt me."

Dammit. How can it see?

The tentacles wave wildly in the air, and when I look closely I see tiny holes—nostrils—on the tip of each appendage. Smelling its way through the world. Monitoring my every move. The broom was worth a try, at least. "What do you want with me?"

"Keeping the Crosskey safe is my duty. Safe at Sparkstone."

Does it know that I want to run away? I steal a glance at the chewing gum on the ceiling, covering the camera. This creature—and whomever it works for—must have realized that I covered its precious view into my private quarters. I'm not sure what's worse: knowing that the school monitors everyone on campus, or the idea that the gross blob creature can watch me while I sleep.

It all seems too outrageous, too . . . pulp-science-fiction-from-the-fifties to believe.

"What's a Crosskey?"

"You are. But . . ." It slurps and gurgles some more as it sticks out a thick, meaty tongue to taste the air. " . . . gene is dormant, Mistress says. I tell Mistress you are sleeping, not awake and not ready for phase four yet."

"Phase four? Who is this Mistress you keep talking about? Tell me!" I step forward, as close as I dare. I don't want to become ensnared in the creature's tentacles.

If the thing wants to kill me it probably would have done so already, and if I am useful to this "Mistress," maybe I can use this as leverage.

"Crosskey does not speak that way to Ohz. But Ohz likes Crosskey's . . . how do you say . . . spirit." The tentacles float towards me and wrap around my arms and legs, leaving a slimy residue on my skin. I squirm and leap back against the closet door, trying to wipe away the grossness, wanting to run away, wishing I could sink into the ground, desiring only to stab the broom handle through the icky creature and see it die horribly on the bedroom floor.

"Crosskey does not like Ohz's touch. I not harm the Crosskey. Ever." It sounds both amused, and disappointed. "Maybe Crosskey likes other form."

Its body blurs, as if an artist is photoshopping the creature in real time. The body odour intensifies as parts of the creature are erased and redrawn. Then: a nose, eyes, a smaller mouth, a face—a face that I recognize. Fleshy lumps become smooth and morph into human skin and human clothes, a one-piece navy jumpsuit that looks as if it hasn't been washed in days. I try to slink back, into the closet, but the door strains against me, and my hands are too sweaty to open it, too busy holding the broom. I won't turn my back on him, not now.

The man clucks his tongue and runs it along his yellow front teeth. "Human speech is much easier to get around in this form, ma'am?"

I clutch the broom tighter. "You're the guard, from the gate. And you were by the greenhouse earlier . . . "

"I can be many things, whatever pleases the Crosskey. The hafelglob, we are known to please. Ask anyone in the galaxy, they'll say, 'Yes ma'am, hafelglob, experts in pleasure.' Pick a form, Crosskey, and Ohz will take it, keep Crosskey safe . . . and warm . . . "

The air around the creature becomes hazy again. While the creature's form is in flux, I seize the opportunity. I ram the tip of the broom handle into the swirling, transforming liquid-gas-solid alien.

Many things happen at once.

Like a giant pimple, part of the creature bursts and spews slimy yellow-green pus everywhere—all over my bedspread, all over the floor, the window—and worst of all, it drenches my front, including my boots.

Now it's personal.

Before I can take another swing, the creature touches a silver band wrapped around the base of one of his shorter, fatter tentacles and fades into nothingness. Almost nothingness—I can hear it sloshing about the room, creating more of a slug-trail and draining more pus everywhere. I swing the broom handle blindly, missing each time. The door creaks open and slams shut just as quickly. He's a fast bugger when he's invisible.

That slimy bastard won't get away, not today.

I throw open the door and swing the broom again. This time I hit something solid, but the cry isn't alien. It's . . . human?

"Don't move," says a disembodied female voice.

I hear raspy breathing, then footsteps—whoever is invisible is running away from me, following the trail of slime down the hallway. About halfway down, the trail stops. It sounds as if someone is punching a whoopee cushion, and then pus explodes all over the walls. The smell of rotten eggs and unwashed armpits and garbage hits my nostrils so forcefully that I fight the urge to throw up again and lose. There's still something in my stomach to spill, it seems. My vomit spreads all over the hallway floor, and I try not to think about it mixing with the alien pus.

"Are you all right?" The voice is closer now. Dainty footsteps press into the pus.

I hold up the broom in defence. Just because this invisible woman beat up a creepy alien doesn't mean she's friendly. "Show yourself."

I blink and there's Jia, standing in the middle of the stench and alien guts. Concern mars her features, and her clothes, like mine, are covered in yellow-green pus.

Jia beat up that alien? But how? She's so small . . .

A more important question leaves my lips instead. "You're one of them, aren't you?"

Jia shakes her head. "I'm not a hafelglob. I'm human."

A human who can turn invisible?

My dream of being on a science fiction show is becoming more of a reality by the moment, but all I want to do is have a hot shower and get rid of my sense of smell.

"Okay," I say slowly. "If you're human, how can you go invisible?"

Jia casually wipes some of the slime off her face, as if she's wiping off something not gross, as if she does this every day. "Ever since . . . ever since I was twelve, I could slip away. I don't know why." She reaches into her pocket and pulls out something sharp. A pocket knife. She flicks the blade open and I instinctively draw away.

She looks worried again. "No, no, I don't want to hurt you. I just have to prove . . . "

Without flinching, Jia draws the knife across the underside of her arm, below her wrist. I cringe as a deep line of blood clots and drips on the floor. But Jia, she is collected. Determined.

"Do you believe me, that I'm human?" she asks.

I can't stop staring at the knife and the blood. "Why would you do that to yourself? Of course I believe you! I didn't say that I didn't."

Jia seems to relax, but only a little. "I had to prove it to you."

"Why?"

"Because I need you to trust me. To trust *us*."

The words hit me hard. They *need* me to trust them. So far they've put themselves in harm's way just to keep me safe. To earn my trust. But why?

"You mean you need me to trust Sunni and Misty and Wil." I inhale sharply, because the next question is hard to ask. "Are they . . . like you?"

Is Ethan?

"It's not safe to talk about here." She presses firmly on her wound. "If the hafelglob are already after you, then we have to move quickly before the Collective sends more."

"The Collective? What's that? And wait . . . there are more of those things? Shouldn't we clean this stuff up?"

"Someone else will clean it up. Right now"—Jia offers me her hand—"we have to move."

"Are you going to explain this to me when we're safe?" I ask.

"Yes. We all will. Please, Ingrid." Her dark almond eyes are begging now. "Do you trust me?"

"I . . . " It's all too much at once. "You saved my life. So . . . yes."

"Good. Because without you, we could all die. Come on!"

CHAPTER 6

"But where—?"

Blink. And she's gone. No sound effects, no fading, just snuffed out of existence. I stand there, frozen, unable to believe that Jia was there only seconds before.

I'm starting to think that maybe this is all one strange dream when Jia pops back into existence again.

"Sorry. I'm used to . . . well, usually, they offer their hands." She grasps my wrist and takes a deep breath. In, and then out. "This might feel . . . strange."

A cold, tingling sensation sweeps over me, the same one you might get when stepping into a freezer after sitting in a sauna. And then, I'm transported to a layer of reality that exists unnoticed within my own world. The real world whistles around me, a constant storm that I don't see when I'm visible to the naked eye. The surroundings blur and drip like a painting that's been splashed with water. I fear touching the floor in case I smudge the carpet or worse, fall through it. Gone is the grime and the dust and the silence. Everything about the hallway sings, and it's beautiful.

When I'm unseen, I see the beauty in everything.

"I know, it was like that the first time for me too," Jia says in an echoey voice. She smiles at my delight. Her skin shines like a pearl and blends with the creamy texture of the wall. "Sometimes I wish I could live here, like this, forever."

"Why don't you?" I ask, and my voice sounds as if it's in an empty room that stretches for miles. We still haven't left the corridor.

She laughs a little bit, and it's like music. A song in D major, and my fingers instantly position themselves, ready to play. If only we weren't chasing aliens, I would have composed the greatest song ever in that moment.

"It's too much after a while," she says finally. "It's paradise. A siren's song. Too dangerous for me to remain here long."

Someone is coming down the hallway. Jia digs her fingernails into my wrist and we stop running. The man's features are blurred, but as he gets closer, I recognize him: it's Wil. I look to Jia because I'm not in control of our visibility. She stares at him, waiting.

He treads carefully down the hall, scanning the ceiling. Three cameras above us whir to life and point at him. He's someone suspicious that needs to be watched, it seems.

But not for long.

The cameras power down. The red recording lights flicker off. Only then does Jia let go of my hand, and we return to the visible world.

"We've got about ninety seconds," Wil says.

I blink. He's not even surprised that we just materialized out of a beautiful nowhere.

"Why only ninety?" Jia asks. "Usually—"

"This isn't usual. We've run into at least ten of those blobs in the past five minutes. They're doing something, all around the school, and I can't . . . " He finally notices I'm there. His dark eyes shift from Jia to me. "Hello . . . "

"Hi," I say. Because there's not much else to say. I'm determined to remain in control, to not freak out, to show that I can handle weird and strange, because I like weird and strange.

Wil frowns. "How much do you know?"

"There are aliens in the school, you guys have special X-Men powers, and . . ." *And Sunni has a mysterious notebook with beautiful poetry and a face I recognize.* " . . . and do you guys hear that sound?"

A melody, barely perceptible, drifts through my ears. I hadn't noticed it before because it blended so well with the background, and while we were in the invisible world, everything was so stimulating that I thought the music was part of the deal.

Wil and Jia listen for a moment but then Wil shakes it off. "Whatever these blobs are planning, it's happening soon. They're in pairs or in threes all over campus, and Misty's going around to the places I've pinpointed but . . ."

He inhales sharply and drags us towards the hallway exit. "I can't hold off anymore. We have to get out of here."

"What's wrong?" I ask as I follow them.

"The cameras," Jia whispers. "He shuts them down, with his mind, but dealing with the blobs, it's too much for him to handle at once."

"Outside," Wil says curtly, heading for the nearest exit. "A bit safer there, to talk at least."

The music is getting louder. There's a repetitiveness to the measures and an urgency to the notes that clutches my heart and makes the hair on my arms rise.

Misty's leaning against the building a few feet away, in the shadows of the evening sun. Her short, black hair whips around her face as we approach, and she evaluates us as a threat. She gives me a dark look and grinds her teeth.

"What's *she*—"

"Doesn't matter. Did you get those blobs?"

"Yeah. Three in the girls' dorm, four more over there. All of them, wearing the same orange construction vests."

"There's been a lot of maintenance around here lately," Jia remarks. "What are they up to?"

"The past few days, I've felt increased electrical energy throughout the campus," Wil says.

"So are they installing something, or does the electrical energy have anything to do with their physiology?" Jia asks.

Wil massages his left temple. "Not sure yet. Maybe Sunni will know. We'll ask her when she gets back."

"The . . . blobs didn't seem to be electrically charged," I say.

They continue their conversation as if I'm not there. The simple musical tune resonates more loudly now, and my foot taps absently in time. The repetitious nature of the tune is drilling into my mind. It's getting faster by a half-beat with every eighth repetition. And it's getting louder. I could whisper and not hear myself, that's how loud it is.

"They're up to something." Wil runs a hand over his smooth, shaved head. "I've never seen anything like them before. They don't belong to the Collective."

"WHAT'S THE COLLECTIVE?" I shout over the song.

The three of them give me strange looks. Can't they hear what I hear?

"We'll explain as soon as we figure out what these blobs are up to, all right?" Jia says.

She starts to say something else, but I plug my ears. Their conversation is muffled, but the mysterious tune marches on. Up the scale, down for a bit, then up—it's definitely in A minor, but it's got a deep-purple C natural in there too. I don't think my synaesthesia has ever acted up this much before. Usually I enjoy tunes in both these keys—the deep, rich colours they invoke are soothing and creamy like butter. But these colours, they're spoiled and rancid. When the C chord finishes out and transitions back into the dark, blood-red tones of A minor, the volume shoots up to deafening heights.

I might lose my hearing because of something no one else can hear. I can't stand the thought of being a deaf musician.

No, not after all the training I've done.

76

Misty's moving her lips and speaking in her harsh, clipped tone. "They could be attackin' Sunni right now, and she's defenceless."

"Sunni can take care of herself. I don't sense she's in any danger."

At least, I think that's what Wil's saying.

Misty spits at his foot. "We shouldn't have left her alone at the café. I'm gonna find her now."

The music is unbearable. I can't stand it any longer. "Wait!" I cry.

Jia, Wil and Misty stop their chattering and look at me. "What's your problem?" Misty demands.

"Something's wrong," I say.

The musical sequence cuts through the air. *Can't they hear it?* From the confused, oblivious looks on their faces, I see that they are deaf to the threat in the measure. I sing along with the tune as it descends the scale. "The music . . . it's getting faster . . . it almost sounds like a countdown."

"What music? A countdown to what?" Wil asks.

And then it all falls into place. The workers in the orange construction vests all over campus—fixing thermostats, standing on ladders pretending to work—all of them, installing little black, beeping boxes.

My heart pounds more loudly than the music. "Bombs."

CHAPTER 7

"I don't hear nothin'," Misty says. "She's crazy."

"You're one to talk," Wil mutters, or at least I think that's what he says. "Tell me what's going on, Ingrid. I promise we'll believe you, however strange it sounds."

I start to tell Wil about the blob in my room, and the tune the alien was humming while installing his black box by the greenhouse, but the music keeps breaking my focus. My throat is closing—there's just so much *there*, filling my ears, my lungs, my head. Another few minutes and there will be nothing left of me.

"Why can she hear it and we can't?" Misty asks.

"I don't know," Wil says. "And that's bad. But maybe it doesn't matter. We have to shut down those boxes."

"How long do we have?" Jia asks.

"Not . . . not long," I say. It's a struggle to talk. "It's . . . so . . . loud. And fast. Louder and . . . faster . . . " My eyes feel hot with tears. I'm ready to die. "Please . . . "

"May I?" Wil places his hands inches from my cheeks. "If I can get a sense of what's going on in your brain, I might be able to turn down the sound and hear it myself."

I nod and blink away tears. I have no other options. "Vulcan mind meld?"

"Not really. More like running a diagnostic on a piece

of malfunctioning software. Except the brain is more like hardware. Anyway, you get the point."

His hands are warm as they cup my face. I grit my teeth. The repetitive string of notes echoes in my mind. My eardrums are ready to explode.

"I'm just trying to find . . . ah! Got it." His eyes snap open. "The music you hear, Ingrid, is on a frequency that for whatever reason . . . it's almost like it's tuned for your brain specifically."

I find this really hard to believe, even though it's not the craziest thing that's happened today. The alien music subsides and descends like the final notes of an orchestra's long concerto. My ears ring, but this time, it's with relief. The tune is still present, but it's in the back of my mind now, simmering and more of a memory than a destructive force.

Hopefully whatever damage this alien tune has caused isn't permanent.

"That better?" he asks. "I've told the synapses in your brain to relax when it comes to this particular string of musical notes, so they don't go firing off all over the place again. It should hold. But if it doesn't, let me know."

I nod, rubbing my ears. They burn as if they've been frostbitten. "How would the tune be for my brain wave specifically? Is that even possible?"

"I don't know. The Collective has access to technology that's much more advanced than ours," Wil explains. "And the tune. There's something about it. Like Ingrid said, a countdown." He adjusts his thin-framed glasses. He's speaking more quickly now, as if he's just made a new scientific discovery. "Music is mathematical. The song is getting faster and louder every eight iterations but there's a hidden note in there that occurs on the thirteenth iteration. That, combined with—"

Misty looks ready to explode. "Would you skip the math lesson and just tell us?"

"Fine," Wil says. "If we don't disable the bombs in two

hours, everyone on campus, maybe everyone in town, is going to die."

The news settles over us like a heavy blanket. Two hours. That's barely enough time to do anything. Misty's hands are fists, and she's glaring at me as if I'm the terrorist. Jia surveys the campus and the few students rushing to Rogers Hall for the tail end of supper. Wil folds his arms and sags his shoulders, as if the weight of his realization is his burden to bear alone.

"What are we going to do?" I say, because no one else is saying anything.

They're all looking at me now. *Sunni said she dreamt that I was coming. Maybe I'm responsible for this. Maybe the aliens are after me.*

"We have to find each bomb box and destroy it," Jia says.

"There could be boxes all over campus!" I exclaim.

"Ingrid's right," Wil says. "It's not efficient for us to run around and try to find them all, however many there are, even with our . . . abilities."

"Well, if you're so *smart*, why don't you figure it out then?" Misty spins on her heels. "I'm going to see if Sunni's all right. She should be in her room by now. Or at the greenhouse, waiting."

"Misty, we should really stick together," Jia says. "What if more of those things come back?"

Misty waves her off and runs towards the girls' dorms. "I have to know she's all right."

Wil heaves a sigh. "Leave her then. She can blast them. We have Jia to keep us out of sight. Right?"

Misty's fire and ice blazes before my mind. *Maybe she shouldn't leave our sides, if she's the one who can actually do some serious damage to them without getting pus all over her clothes.* The alien slime-pus has dried somewhat on my skirt but has left unpleasant stains on my long-sleeved shirt.

"The blobs are blind," I say. "They smell us with those tentacles of theirs, I guess. But they also have cloaking

80

abilities. So . . . I guess we can see them when they're invisible, if we're invisible too?"

"Not exactly, but I can see their outline more clearly," Jia replies.

"That's not our biggest problem. We have to find out how many bombs they've placed." Wil rubs his temples, thinking. "The tune you heard is in my head now. If it really is some kind of countdown, I might be able to put it into a central computer to help locate all the boxes. I can feel some of them—they're all over campus—but there are too many of them for me to hold in my head at one time. There must be a central location that powers and controls all the bomb boxes . . . "

He mutters to himself and paces the grass. I tap my fingers against the brick wall of the building while Jia keeps a watchful eye on the horizon.

"Is there some sort of security room, where we can access the cameras? We might be able to spot all the boxes that way," I say.

"There is a central computer that controls the security feed," Wil says. "It's in the security room, next to Professor Jadore's office, in MacLeod Hall. But the security room is only accessible *through* Jadore's office."

I pull the curls around my face, hard enough that it hurts and this confirms that yes, what is happening is real. We have two hours to sneak into Jadore's office and disable a series of bombs that could destroy everything and everyone at Sparkstone.

"Is she in her office now?" Jia asks Wil.

His eyebrows furrow as he concentrates. "I feel her in that general direction, yeah. We don't have a choice, we have to find a way in."

Jia holds out a porcelain hand to each of us. Her eyes are bleary, as if she's just spent twelve hours staring at a bright computer screen. Her ability to make us invisible must be taxing on her. But she doesn't complain. Her lips are set in a determined line. Wil takes her hand first, and for a moment he looks like a weary solider who has had to save the world one too many times. I wonder if this is the first time something like this has happened, if I'm the first person who has stumbled upon their clique and uncovered their extraordinary powers.

My fingers clasp Jia's cold hand, and when we're certain no one is looking, we dissolve into her watery, invisible world. Wil leads the charge towards MacLeod Hall. None of us speak, but I see wheels turning in Wil's mind. He's making a plan. I wonder if I should dare to speak, to contribute to the heist.

If Jadore's door is closed, how are we supposed to open it without arousing suspicion? Jadore's blind, so will being invisible really help us?

Jia and Wil don't seem like the kind of people who take chances.

Inside MacLeod Hall, the air is cool. I tiptoe because on the tile, my boots are a lot louder than Wil's sneakers and Jia's slip-ons. To my left, down the hallway where we had our tutorial today, a few students are lounging on the floor by the large windows across from the classrooms. Directly in front of us is a set of double doors with tinted windows. Wil pulls Jia towards a hallway off to the far right and Jia stumbles forward. I lose my balance just as I notice Ethan coming through the set of double doors.

My hand slips from Jia's, and suddenly, I'm visible. I catch myself before I fall flat on my face, but the noise I make is enough to draw Ethan's attention.

"Oh! Ingrid," Ethan says, blinking and shaking his head in surprise. "Sorry, you snuck up on me a bit there."

Yeah. More than you know. My heart is pounding. *Does he suspect? No, he couldn't.* My eyes trail around the room, searching for where Jia and Wil might have gone. "Hey . . . "

"You're all set for tonight? I'm about to head over. I'll be ready for you in about an hour or so."

"An hour? Yeah, that sounds good." I don't know what else to say, except, *We'll all be dead in two hours if I don't stop aliens from blowing up the school.* Backing out of our plans to meet is too hard right now, and seems too pessimistic.

"Brilliant." He smiles. "I'll see you in an hour."

We share a long look as he strides down the hallway and out the door.

That could have been the last time I ever speak to him. And I wasted the opportunity to say something more meaningful.

Not only that, my clothes are filthy, and I smell as if I haven't showered in weeks.

A hand grabs my wrist, and then I'm back in the fluid, liquid world of the invisible.

"What did you do that for?" Jia demanded, her usually calm voice on edge. "There are cameras! We don't want Jadore to catch us before we even get to her office."

"Sorry, my hand slipped."

Wil leads us down the right hallway, deeper into enemy territory. "You're not really going to meet him in an hour, are you?"

Jia puts a finger to her lips. "Shh. Let's just focus on this."

We manoeuvre around a handful of students walking through the narrow hallway. This wing is all offices, and each door has a gold nameplate detailing the name of the professor and his or her teaching speciality and what tutorial he or she is in charge of. The ethnicities of the names ranges like the professions. They've got every career possible crammed into this narrow hallway, from mechanical engineering to journalism to art history to astrophysics. Some professors have two or three specifications listed beneath their names. I wonder if they're aware of the science fiction show happening around them, or if like me, they were lured here with the promise of an elite, learned atmosphere.

Wil points to Jadore's office, and my courage sinks into my toes. The door has a gold nameplate that reads: *Professor Sistrine Jadore. Astrophysics, Psychiatry, Psychology, Biochemistry. Tutorial 16.* The door is ajar and the conversation within spills into the hallway.

" . . . a mistake."

"Everything is on track. Unless you believe my leadership is incompetent—"

"No, I am not questioning that. However . . . "

Jia puts a finger to her lips as we scuttle to a stop. I lean over and peek through. Ms. Agailya paces the room, her flowing skirts trailing as she saunters. Jadore sits at her desk in front of her dual monitor computer. Leaning against the desk is Jadore's walking cane. Behind her, the curtains draping the window are shut, but a touch of the setting sun's light seeps through.

We should wait until they're gone, Wil says to our minds.

My eyes widen, and not just because his voice is in my head. We don't have time to wait. We've got less than two hours until everyone on campus is toast. They could be in there for hours!

Wil reads my expression and gestures to the door, as if to say, *Be my guest, go in there and distract them.* I shake my head.

Jadore is talking again. "The benefits outweigh the risks. Having them on this project is paramount to our success."

"How?" Ms. Agailya demands in her silvery voice. "The students are sentient. They do feel. Introducing the hafelglob into this is nothing more than—"

"I've heard enough!" Jadore slams her fist on her desk, sending a jolt of fear through the three of us. "I am in charge of the Crosskey project, Agailya. Bringing up the humans' emotions is hardly an argument for protecting them, especially coming from you. Don't think I don't know about your own *side project.* Remember why we are here. I only wish to speed the Harvest along, and the hafelglob will help us do that. I will continue as planned, unless you wish to make a formal complaint about my methods to the council."

My eyes are practically bugging out of my head. Does this mean that Jadore and Ms. Agailya are aliens in disguise too?

And more importantly, what does Jadore mean when she says *the Harvest*?

"My *side project* is condoned by the council and fits within the Sparkstone mandate it has set forth. This is a perfect environment to test the equations. And the tests are going well, and they meet the standards of the Ethics Board." She spins and heads for the door. "I do not oppose you, Jadore. I am loyal to the Collective. But I do warn you. We are not as weak as we are stereotyped to be."

I press myself against the wall as Ms. Agailya opens the door and walks past us. She barely makes a sound as she glides down the hallway.

"Insolence," Jadore mutters. She types something on her computer.

I shrug at Wil. *How are we supposed to get inside if she's not going to leave?*

Wil takes a small step forward and raises his forefinger. He points it through the crack in the door. *I'm sorry, lil guy.*

I don't know what he's talking about until I hear a small explosion. Jadore spews a string of foreign profanities as she leaps out of her chair. I strain to see what's going on, but then she's right at the door. Jia pulls Wil out of the way just as Jadore flies out of the room and down the hallway, muttering about human technology and its incompatibility with her superior machines.

When she's gone, Jia, Wil, and I sneak into the office and shut the door. Wil kills the camera in the right hand corner of the room. Tufts of black smoke billow up from Jadore's computer tower, and the smell of burnt plastic fills the air. Jia releases us from the invisible world and collapses in Jadore's office chair as if she's just run a marathon.

And I'm just standing in the middle of it all, the alien music whispering in the back of my mind.

"This is really crazy," I say.

Wil touches the security room doorknob and it clicks open. "That confirms it. Jadore is a member of the Collective—some sort of high-ranking leader, maybe on the council—and Ms. Agailya is working for them too."

Jia rubs her face. "That's too bad. I really liked Ms. Agailya. I really thought . . . " She shakes her head and looks away, lost in thought.

In the security room—barely bigger than a walk-in closet—Wil finds the light and sits down before sixteen TV monitors, in rows of four by four. The black-and-white screens show feeds from the cameras around the school. There are a few computers hooked up as well, and on top of them are the same black boxes that I saw the blobs installing.

"Look!" I say.

Wil's hand hovers over them. "Yeah. This seems to be . . ." He kneels and then studies one of the boxes from every possible angle. "I feel it. It's collecting readings from sixteen different sources around the school, and it's definitely the one sending the signal, but . . . it also seems to be sending another signal, somewhere else . . . "

He starts muttering technobabble to himself. Jia looks ready to fall asleep. I crack open the door to make sure Jadore's not going to come waltzing back in. Questions are boiling inside me and they have to be answered.

"What's the Collective?" I ask.

Jia opens her eyes with a pained expression on her face and glances at Wil, who is too busy with the equipment to answer. She sighs, long and slow. "It's a group of aliens that control Sparkstone."

"Like the university, or the whole town?"

"Both . . . potentially," she replies. "We've suspected for a while now that Jadore is an alien. It's easier to assume that all of the professors are aliens or working for the Collective in some way, until we find evidence that they're not. As for the town, we just assume that anyone who doesn't bleed red is an alien."

My heart pounds hysterically. I keep my gaze focussed on the hallway. "The way Ms. Agailya was talking, it sounds like she's a different kind of alien than Jadore. How many different kinds of aliens are there?"

"Dozens. Probably more we don't even know about."

"How don't you know? Haven't you been here for at least a month?"

"Yeah, but . . . " Wil looks uncomfortable. "This is the first time we've seen them clearly, up close. They must really want you bad if they were willing to risk blowing their human cover. And these . . . hafelglob . . . we've never seen them before today."

Just thinking about the hafelglob's rows of teeth and the trail of slime it left on the bedroom floor and its tentacles wrapping around my arms gives me the creeps.

"They're the ones planting the bombs. You think Jadore ordered them to do that?" I frown. "But why? If Sparkstone University is supposed to be some experiment for them, why would she want to blow it up?"

"We should save the *why* for later," Wil says. He gestures us into the security room. "We've got a bigger problem here."

"Can you shut down the bomb signal?" Jia asks.

Wil sighs and kneels before the computer tower that plays host to the alien black box. "This box isn't exactly the source. It's accepting and transmitting information to all the bomb boxes around campus. Destroying it would theoretically stop the detonation. But it's not the detonator."

"Can't we destroy it to buy some time?" The music hums hauntingly in my mind.

"We could, but then someone might notice we've tampered with it and set off the explosion."

Jia clasps her hands. "So where is the detonator? Do you know, Wil?"

Wil looks up at the ceiling. "I feel like the signal is pointing upward. Maybe on the roof. Or maybe . . . just maybe . . . "

"Just maybe what?" I ask.

Wil's attention snaps to the door. "Jadore's coming back."

Jia grabs our arms and we fall back into her invisible, silvery world. I pull us towards the window and open the curtains. My hand moves across the fabric and creates a trail of beige and blue. We're on the first floor so it's not a long way down, but there are three of us, and only one window. I thrust the window up and Wil, his large hand hiding Jia's fingers in his palm, goes out first.

Jadore's footsteps are closer now, and her cane thunks on the hardwood in the hallway. It melds with the faint bomb tune in my head, in time with the offbeat, and creates a melody that, if I weren't invisible and trying to escape from a dangerous situation, would've inspired me to compose something on the spot.

Jia's climbing over the sill now, dragging me with her. If I let go, I'll become visible, but she can't let go of Wil, who is outside, because there are students milling around campus. We've been pretty lucky so far, but if one of the students sees us appear out of nowhere, it would only add to the craziness swirling around campus.

I straddle the sill as Wil holds Jia around her legs. It's hard to manoeuvre myself when I'm wearing this skirt and Jia's got my hand. I curse my bulky—but still awesome—boots for their awkwardness. I bring my other leg around and slide myself down under the sill as the office door bursts open and Jadore slips inside.

I freeze. My left hand grips the sill tighter. I know she can't see me. She's blind, and I'm invisible, but Jadore hesitates at the threshold.

A splinter digs into my palm and I bite my lip to calm my agony. Jadore's cane thumps against the floor—*thump, thump, thump*—three times, and then she's at the open window.

Do not move. Do not speak. Do not do ANYTHING.

The curtains flutter in the breeze as a copper hand rests on the sill. *Oh no—I forgot, the curtains were closed before, but now, they're open! Does she know?* I can't tell what she's looking at because her sunglasses are reflective, but her head tilts slightly, looking up, left, right, and then down. My grip strains. I'm invisible, she can't see me, but she looks right at me . . .

. . . and then disappears from the window.

Did she see me?

"Let go!" Jia whispers.

I do, and together we drop to the ground. Jia lands on her feet like a cat but I stumble and fall forward. We pop back into the visible world, and all I want to do is sleep.

"You all right?" Wil whispers. He helps me to my feet.

"Fine," I say. My skirt has some grass stains but they are nothing compared to the crusted alien slime. I brush off my skirt. "Do you see or sense anything on the roof?"

Wil strides away from MacLeod Hall, towards the front of the building. He strains to look at the ceiling. "I don't see anything. Don't really sense anything either. Has the music changed at all?"

The tune is louder—not as loud as it was before—but it's more frantic. I'm about to describe it when I spot Misty running across the campus. She dodges clumps of trees and yells Wil's and Jia's names. The people milling about the campus like ants, with no idea that their lives are at stake, regard her with curious looks and continue on their courses. Jia rushes towards her and Wil and I follow.

Misty skids to a stop as she looks at the three of us. "Where's Sunni?"

"Weren't you just going to find her, in her room?" I ask.

"Shut your hole, this is effin major," Misty spits. "If she's not with you . . . "

"Finding Sunni can wait. We have a bigger problem. The detonator isn't here. I'm not even sure if it's on campus at all," Wil says.

"If it's not on campus . . ." Jia trails off.

"Shut *up* about the effin bombs. *Tell me* where Sunni is!"

Misty's fists burn with the power of fire and ice as she grabs Wil by his shirt collar. Even though he's almost a foot taller than she is, she lifts him off the ground. Wil's shirt burns from Misty's fiery touch and then freezes stiff.

"Use your mind power," Misty hisses.

Jia tugs on Misty's arm. "Stop this. There are people watching."

A few students look over nervously at Misty and start to whisper. She throws them dangerous *don't-mess-with-me* glares.

"Screw them."

But Misty does set him down. I look around. There aren't that many people around, but the ones who caught wind of the disturbance have already moved on. Wil straightens his collar and then closes his eyes, concentrating.

"She's . . . " He frowns. "No, that's not right."

"Tell me what's wrong." Misty's voice is on the verge of hysteria.

Wil opens his eyes and looks at the setting sun. "She *was* in her room . . . "

"I already looked there, and the botany lab, and the greenhouse, and—"

"I said was. And there's something else there now. Something not human."

That's all Misty needs to know. "We shouldn't have ever left her alone!"

She's off again, heading back from where she'd come, towards Rita House. Wil runs after her.

"I don't know if I should go," I say. "If this is another fight, I don't think I'll be much use. Plus, the bombs—"

"Sunni believes you're like us," Jia says, grabbing my hand. We slip into her safe, invisible world and she begins pulling me across the campus.

"Like you? But I don't have any sort of superpower!" I protest quietly as we pass a group of freshmen girls, who blur into the air as if someone is erasing them with a thumb.

"Sunni's dreams don't lie," Jia replies. "She predicted that another would come, and she described you, right down to those boots you're wearing. And you can hear the tune that the explosives emit. Maybe your power is similar to Wil's."

I don't reply because I don't really want to encourage the conversation. Okay, I do want to encourage it . . . a little. But it's dangerous. The moment I start thinking I have special abilities is the moment I stop focussing on what is important—school—and start running around with crazy people trying to fight aliens.

Well, I guess I'm already on my way to failing university.

We follow Misty and Wil into Rita House and up the stairs towards Sunni's dorm. Some of the girls we pass give Wil really strange looks—a six-foot-tall man running for his life through a hallway he's not really supposed to be in would arouse suspicion in anyone, but he's too fast to catch up with, so we can't absorb him into Jia's invisible world.

Two black boxes are stuck to the ceiling above Sunni's room that weren't there before. The alien tune spikes in my mind, as if someone has suddenly turned up the volume.

Sunni's door is wide open. Wil and Misty run through the threshold first and stop immediately. Jia lets go of me, and we're both gasping for breath.

There are three hafelglob in Sunni's bedroom, and the carpet is completely soaked with slime. It clings to

Wil's sneaker as he lifts his foot with disgust. The alien blobs appear to be unarmed, but they are wearing shiny metal bands around their middles. One is plopped on Sunni's bed, smearing itself over the footboard. Another is sliming up against her fish tank. The third is stuck to the far wall, installing a black box behind a bookshelf sagging with biology texts.

They stop their suckling noises and perk up when we enter. Misty's cheeks are a deep shade of red. I flinch as she readies a fireball. The aliens' tentacles sniff the air hesitantly as the room heats up. The one attached to the wall propels itself onto the bed and then onto the floor. I see it more clearly now: there's a large, angry puncture wound in its side, and it's got splotchy black bruises all over its body. It's the guard from the gate—or as he called himself, Ohz.

"Where's Sunni?" Misty demands.

Ohz gurgles in what I'm sure is a laugh. "Fire-girl wants the Sunni-girl? Come and find her. If Fire-girl can."

The other hafelglob laugh it up. Misty growls at them like a wronged mother bear and throws a ball of white-hot flames at them. They press the button on the metal bands and the fire passes right through them. They're fading into nothing, going back to wherever they came from.

This doesn't stop Misty. She lunges for them but it's too late. They're gone. Screaming her lungs out, she kicks the baseboard of Sunni's bed. I'm afraid that she'll start grabbing Sunni's pillows and find her journal that I wasn't supposed to read, so I grab her arms to steady her.

"Get off me!" she screams, but she doesn't resist my grip. She wants to be hugged, I think, but no one will chance it. The sparks jumping from her hands are too much of a risk. I let go of her and she stands there, a bubbling rage. "We have to get her back. We have to."

"We'll find her," I say, even though I have no idea how. I'm definitely not the authority on these matters, no matter how many alien TV shows I've watched. I check my cell phone. We have little over an hour until everyone on campus explodes.

I'm in way over my head.

PART TWO

Death does not concern me, but rather, Time. Worshipped by some and abhorred by others, I am trapped within her clutches, while I await the Crosskey, who will deliver me from my insanity.

—J.G.C., from *Campbell's Multiple Verses*

Earth is too beautiful, too small in the endless black vacuum of space to look at. And yet Sunni can't tear away her gaze.

She's been on this bridge before, in her dreams. She has felt the impossibly thick, warm glass against her palms, the rumbling pulse of the spaceship's engines, and she's breathed in the recycled oxygen. The consistency of the scene from one moment to the next as Sunni inhales and exhales her fears is the only indication that she isn't dreaming now.

She will never set foot in Texas again. Mama will cry and wonder where she is, just like the time she sobbed for months and months and sat in that room by the stairs, with one eye on the road and one eye on the pond. At least with Daddy, they knew the risks. When he left, there was always the chance he wasn't coming back.

Mama didn't know the risks when she allowed Sunni to go to Sparkstone. But Sunni did. She accepted them, gladly, especially when Misty told her she'd been accepted to Sparkstone as well. Sunni never would have let Misty enter the lair of the beast alone.

She will never say goodbye to her closest friends but thinks it might be better this way. Misty knows the harsher side of life, but Wil and Jia—Sunni knows they can see a light at the end of all of this. Once she'd even seen Jia, years older, with a young child. Successful. Happy.

But Ingrid, poor Ingrid. She will find out what she really is, and her purpose. It's not Sunni's place to tell Ingrid that a normal life is a twinkling star in her eyes, a far-off dream in her head. Not tonight, anyway.

Tonight is the night she's been dreaming of for weeks. On this bridge, on this starship orbiting the planet Earth, she is going to die.

Sunni sits cross-legged on the grated floor and begins to meditate. It is the only thing she can do to calm her nerves. To forget the clickety-clacking of the aliens of all shapes and sizes behind her and below her, working at their stations in the dim yellow and red lighting. To forget she is breathing recycled air. To forget what she knows is about to come.

There is nothing that anyone can do to stop Sunni's dreams from coming to pass. Nothing.

The serpent is coming. Sunni mouths the seconds as she counts down. *Five . . . four . . . three . . . two . . .*

Eyes open. It is her, bathed in shadows, dressed in her true skin: green scales that shimmer as she passes the starlight-filled windows. Her black lips and pointed teeth, pure contrast, and her slithering tongue, forked like the devil's, sliding out to taste the air. "You knew I was coming, didn't you."

Breathe in, breathe out. She will not die in fear. "Yes."

Slowly, gracefully, Sunni rises to her feet like a ballerina about to perform her last dance. Jadore stands two feet away. Sunni doesn't want to count the seconds to her death, but the feeling of déjà vu is creeping up on her with each moment that passes, and there will be a moment soon where it all culminates in one big climax—*la fin*—and she will feel no more.

One moment. Two moments. Jadore tilts her head and the reflection of the sun and the Earth's gentle glow catches her large, black eyes.

"What are you waiting for?" Sunni asks.

"I was just thinking," she says, her *s*'s hissing as they escape her reptilian-humanoid hybrid mouth. "How useful you would be to the Collective, should we keep your heart beating and your mind alive. We can do that, Sunni."

"No, thank you."

"It was not a request." She raises a stiff finger as her nail elongates and sharpens to a point. "You will not fight me, Sunni? Your friends . . . they are not here to protect you?"

They won't get here in time, Sunni thinks. "What friends?"

Jadore's voice is sickly sweet. "Don't play this game. We know there are others, like you. And they all must contribute to our great cause." A cruel smile touches the corners of her lips. Sunni wonders how many Sparkstone students have died here, on this bridge, because of something they couldn't change. "Accept your death if you wish, Sunni Harris, but it will be in vain. We will find your co-conspirators and harvest them when they show themselves, as you have showed yourself to us. Do you accept your death?"

Sunni leans against the alien glass panels, which separate space and the stars from her body, and forces the world to go black. Misty, Wil, Jia, even Ingrid, they will find out everything she knows in time. She didn't tell them the things she'd discovered about Joseph G. Campbell and the Collective and the future she'd seen clearly in her dreams—because if they see the things she sees, and if they knew what she would do if left alive, what the Collective would make her do, what Ingrid and the others would become because of it . . .

No. Sunni can prevent it all. By surrendering to the dream that has plagued her for weeks, to the future that whispers the least harshly in her ear, she can stay the Collective from obtaining her sacred, terrible power.

She will protect her friends, with her death.

CHAPTER 8

The seconds are ticking by, and the bomb's tune is just on the edge of my hearing.

We're all going to die.

Jia and Wil are speaking in frantic whispers about what to do. Wil has blocked the cameras in Sunni's room but it really doesn't seem to matter anymore. "We have to focus on finding the bomb detonator," he's saying.

"But the hafelglob have Sunni, and they also have the campus rigged. There must be a connection."

"We don't have time to focus on connections, we have to find the detonation control—"

"Shut it you two," Misty snaps. Her hands are at the ready, cackling with blue and red energy. "Which way, Wil? Where did they take her?"

Wil closes his eyes again, concentrating. "She's . . . she's not in Sparkstone."

"They couldn't have taken her far," Jia says, but uncertainty shakes her voice.

"I don't know about that," he says, and frowns. "I feel her, a faint signal, but it's far. Really far. As if . . . " He looks up at the ceiling. "No way . . . "

"Oh no," Misty says, backing up against the wall. "You think . . . "

"Has to be. She's on their mother ship."

"In space?" A sense of awe floods me. "But how could they get there so quickly? Do you think they have beaming technology, is that why they disappeared like they did? Even if there's a shuttle somewhere, they'd have to have someplace to hide it . . . "

"The Collective's never taken anyone to their mother ship before! That we know of." Misty absently twists and pulls on the earring in her stretched earlobe. "We have to get her back. We have to."

Jia says what I secretly fear. "She could be dead."

Misty shoots Jia a death stare. "Don't say that. How could you even say that?"

"We have to stay calm and think this through," I say, as swirling twin snakes of fear and anticipation slither inside my stomach. I return Misty's intense stare. "And consider every possibility. I don't know much about these aliens—"

"No, you don't," Misty says flatly.

"—but if the school is being run by them like you say, they must have a way to transport back and forth, from Earth to the mother ship."

"Yeah, they're freakin' aliens. They can transport themselves with the push of a button! We're wasting time. I can't . . . I just can't . . . " She tugs at her hair and screams inside her mouth. Her sanity seems to be walking on a thin tightrope.

Jia approaches Misty as one would approach a distressed viper, and as she moves in to comfort her, Misty lashes out, pushing Jia away. "Stop it. I don't need your *pity*."

"We're all upset," Wil says. "But Ingrid is right. They have to have transport somewhere—for supplies, and junk like that that might be too heavy to teleport with a single person. There's a transport facility somewhere within Sparkstone, and I think I know where it is."

"Then shut up and take me there." A stray tear escapes Misty's eye and rolls down her left cheek, leaving a faint black trail of mascara in its wake. She wipes it away defiantly and whips her hand towards Jia.

Wil crosses his arms. "Jia should save her strength. We'll run."

"Fine by me," Misty mutters, and is already out the door.

Sighing, Wil gives me an apologetic look and starts after her. Jia and I follow them into the hallway and down the stairs.

"How's your head?" Wil asks.

I grit my teeth. "Fine. The music is slowly getting louder again though."

"Hmm." He doesn't look amused. "I was afraid of that."

Ahead, Misty is clambering down the stairs and I hear the door open. The hallways are mostly empty because darkness is falling, and the super smart students of Sparkstone University are probably working on their special projects in their dorms or studying in the library. Wil picks up his pace to catch up with Misty since he's the one who actually knows where we're going. All this running around is giving me cramps but I don't want to seem weak by admitting it.

"Misty must really care a lot about Sunni," I say, because I can't think of anything else to say, and because I want to think about something other than the music in my head.

"They knew each other before they came here," Jia replies. "Misty's always been really protective of Sunni. I think . . . " She frowns but then reconsiders whatever she was going to say and shakes her head. "I know it's easy to hate Misty. And I know it's easy to feel sorry for her too. But if you want her to respect you, you can't do either of those things. It took me a while to realize that. And sometimes, I forget."

I smile a bit as we exit the building. "You're really insightful, you know that, right?"

"I am what I have to be," she says simply.

That quiet warrior look returns to her face, and I wonder

how many encounters with hafelglob and other aliens it will take for me to look like her. I sigh. If I even want to look like her. My desire to focus on school and having a normal life seems to be slipping away with each passing moment.

Outside, the evening chill has settled in. The sun is a thin line of yellow and orange on the horizon, and though street lamps keep Sparkstone fiercely lit, one or two defiant stars still shine through the darkness above. We trek across campus, past Rogers Hall, past MacLeod Hall and the greenhouse. It's a little easier to run across the grassy plains than it is to run on the pavement in my boots. To my right, the town of Sparkstone is settling in for the night. It's eerie: there are hardly any city sounds, like cars honking and people laughing and dogs barking. But there are also no crickets or nature sounds either, and that is more disturbing. We're running out of time.

Time. Oh *no*. Ethan!

I dig out my phone, look up his number, and frantically text him: *Sorry. Can't come tonight. Sunni's friends started watching a movie, wouldn't let me leave. Sorry again. Maybe tomorrow?*

If there is a tomorrow. He has to understand.

Jia notices me texting but doesn't comment. I wonder about her family and her friends back wherever she is from, and if they are worried about her. I wonder about Wil and Misty's families, too, and if they know how special Wil, Misty, Jia, and Sunni are. I imagine Jadore, in her large sunglasses, informing a group of loved ones about our deaths, while the hafelglob mutilate our decomposing corpses only a few feet away.

Maybe some people would survive if Sparkstone explodes. Maybe Ethan would be one of them. Maybe if my parents couldn't, he would avenge my death. I scold myself. *I just blew him off to help my new friends fight an alien attack. He's not going to do me any favours.*

Jia and I catch up with Wil and Misty, and I think about our awkward little quad. I had left friends behind in Calgary. Sure, I'll keep in touch with them online, but I probably won't get upset if I don't see them for months, possibly years. I knew coming here that I'd meet new friends, new people. Misty's steady pace as she runs, the *thump-thump, thump-thump* of her boots as they hit the concrete pathway contains more passion for one person than I'd ever felt for all my friends back home combined.

The soft light in the interior lobby of the tech building is hazy like fog. Above the doors, I can just barely make out the writing on the gold plate: Conrod Building. Conrod Building is isolated from the other structures in Sparkstone. The wall that surrounds the university and the town is maybe forty feet away, and runs along behind the tech building and into the darkness. Conrod Building is larger than any warehouse I've ever seen—almost large enough to fit Rogers Hall, MacLeod Hall, and the four residences inside.

Wil swipes his key card, and with a triumphant beep, the building lets us in. "There shouldn't be too many stragglers in the labs, and even if there are, they'll be too busy. Some of us have projects due next week."

"Let me guess. You're done yours already?" I say.

He smirks. "Three weeks ago."

We barely fit in the narrow lobby. Three boxy elevators sit in front of us, and two doors with keypads stand at attention on either side of us.

"Which way?" Misty cracks her knuckles.

"Beyond the labs." Swiping his key card again, Wil calls an elevator. "There's a restricted area. Mostly storage. Some of us like to play with metals and other materials that would make the general public and other scientists go apecrack if they knew we had them here. Anyway." We pile into the elevator and Wil presses the bottom-level button. The doors shut promptly and I barely feel the jolt of the elevator as it starts to move.

"A few days ago, some of the professors led some men in suits into the lab. Showed them all what we were working on. Supposedly they were CSIS or CIA or something like that, but they had Collective written all over them.

"Down the hall"—the elevator stops and the doors slide open—"that's where they went."

Twenty feet away at the end of the corridor is a set of double doors. A red glow emanates from beneath the doors, emphasized by the lack of light in the hallway.

I'm the first to step out of the elevator. "What's behind that door?"

"The men in suits didn't leave from any other direction. Either there's another exit beyond those doors . . . or the large shuttle that's been whispering to me for the past couple of days actually exists."

Misty cuts in front of Wil and starts down the hallway. "Can you fly it?"

"Maybe," Wil says. "I'm more interested in knowing if Jia can cloak it."

Jia inhales deeply. "I . . . I don't know . . . I've never cloaked something that large before."

"You can already do more than I can," I say, placing a comforting hand on her shoulder. "All of you can."

Jia offers me a small smile. "Sunni thinks you have a gift too. You just have to discover it."

The alien tune flows beneath her words and seems to chirp its agreement. Maybe it wouldn't be such a bad life, to be like them. Becoming invisible, reading the energy off living and non-living things, shooting lethal bursts of fire and ice from my fingertips—the amount of good I could do with any of those gifts, it seems endless.

"Camera!" Jia shouts, pointing to the corner above the door.

"Don't worry. It's been looping since we first stepped into the building," Wil says. He produces his key card again as we approach the door. "Now I don't know if this is going to work. But maybe if I just coax . . . "

He kneels by the door handle, his shaved head leaning comfortably against the polished face of the door.

"What are you doing?" I ask, leaning down beside him. "You can read both people and *things*?"

"It's not that simple," Wil replies. He begins to whisper to the lock. I strain to hear what he's saying, but it just sounds like nonsense. A few seconds later, the lock clicks and the door creaks open. I hold my breath and wait for an alarm to sound. Nothing.

"Each person—each individual thing—emits an energy signature. I'm just tuning in to that frequency."

"Is that how you subdued the music in my brain?"

"Sort of. I tune into the components of things. It's like . . . they speak to me." He wipes his brow. Then, over the alien music, over Jia's nervous nail-tapping on the walls and Misty's restless pacing, I hear Wil's voice in my head. *I can also project my voice like this.*

"Stop showing off," Misty mutters.

Wil leaps up, gently pulls me away from the door, and gestures to Misty. "All yours."

Misty throws the door open. Her touch leaves an icy handprint. Wil and Jia slip inside, but when I try to go through, Misty holds up fiery hand. I feel the heat on my chest and dare not take another step.

"You're not coming."

It's because I'm not like you, isn't it, I want to say. But I won't let Misty have the best of me. "I'm a part of this, just like you."

"No. Those blob things were after *you*. And now they have Sunni because of you. You have nothing that I want to risk my life—or Sunni's life—for. Wil. Give Ingrid your card so she can go back."

But Wil is already halfway into the warehouse, beyond Misty's threatening form. I see a variety of crates stacked high and large white sheets draped over something massive, hidden by shadow and red security lights.

I narrow my eyes. I can't let her scare me. "I'm going. You're right, it probably is my fault that the blobs are here. Which means it's my responsibility to help get Sunni back." I chance a step forward. The fabric of my shirt darkens and burns the skin beneath. My entire outfit, except my boots, is forfeit anyway. I tear up reflexively but refuse to cry out and give Misty the satisfaction of seeing me in pain.

"Let her in, Misty. We're wasting time," Jia says. She looks up at the large white sheet. "Wil . . . why aren't there any—?"

Wil suddenly runs towards us. "Misty, Ingrid, get in here *now!*"

I hear them down the hallway. Loud, squishy, suction sounds and then a *whirr* as they shimmer into existence. The hafelglob. Five, no, six of them. Their tentacles thrash and entangle with one another like brainless lovers, but some wrap around shiny black guns. One fires on Misty and me, and I push her into the open door, right into Wil and Jia, and together we fall to the concrete floor in a tangled, frantic heap.

The now-familiar wave of invisibility washes over me but it's not going to do us much good. We're making too much noise, the four of us trying to find our feet, Jia awkwardly trying to keep our invisibility intact, and the hafelglob, they're squishing and belching and firing red and blue lasers at us. The lasers leave deep black burn marks on the white walls.

"GO!" Misty pushes the three of us towards the massive thing covered in a white sheet.

Wil and Jia don't hesitate. They run. Jia's grip slips from Misty and me and we're exposed. Misty's got this fierce look in her eye. She's hungry for the fight. *Besides Sunni, this is what she loves*, I think, as the slimy aliens slither into the room. Misty unleashes her hellish flames and a cold barrier of ice at them, and a high-pitched war cry from the depths of her stomach fills my ears. That's when

I run. Not because of the deadly laser beams nipping at my heels. Because I'm afraid that if Sunni is right and I am some sort of vigilante with superpowers, I don't want to feel that same hunger, that same anger twisted with desire, that lives in Misty. Right now, I have to distance myself from her, so I am not consumed.

Up ahead, the large sheet falls like an avalanche onto the concrete, revealing what we'd come here for. The shuttlecraft has a flat top and a round underbelly, like a pregnant stingray. It has one visor-like window slashed across its front, but I see no other way in. I chance a glance behind me: the blobs are slowed by Misty's ice and burned by her fire, but more of them are piling into the room, sliding towards her.

With a hiss that bites my ear, the bottom of the shuttlecraft opens, and I hear sounds of someone—I pray it's Wil and Jia—clambering inside. I jump in after them, onto a steel grate.

"We can't just leave her out there," I say.

Wil and Jia shimmer into existence. There are no seats in this shuttlecraft: it clearly wasn't designed for human use. A circular panel outlines half the shuttlecraft under the main view window, which faces a wall. Wil is already tapping buttons and muttering in sweet whispers to the machine to coax it to work under his command.

Jia looks torn. "I have to save my energy. I have to cloak this thing in space so we're not caught."

My stomach clenches. She is willing to sacrifice Misty to save Sunni.

There is an explosion outside the ship, and the scent of burnt flesh and body odor fills the air. My nerves are doing flip-flops. "Misty, your friend, could die out there!"

Jia kneels on the floor, as if she's about to start meditating amidst the chaos. "She knows the risks."

This isn't right. Sunni wouldn't want Misty to die; the risk is too great.

I clamber out of the hatch, and the click of my heels on the concrete floor drives the truth home: I'm the stupid one in this situation. Of course Jia isn't sacrificing Misty to save Sunni. Misty is sacrificing *herself* so that we can save Sunni.

"Get back in here!" Jia shouts.

I not harm the Crosskey. The hafelglob's words turn over in my mind as I run towards the aliens and their gunfire. Tentacles splay in my direction, sensing my presence, and one of them points a gun at me.

"Get away from her!" I shout, reaching for Misty. I hold out my palm, as if I too can shoot fire and ice with only a thought.

At the sound of my voice, the hafelglob cease fire, and even the flame in Misty's palm fizzles out. The hafelglob blurb and gurgle and their tentacles hang in the air, as if they're trying to figure out who I am. But we don't have time to discern what the alien blobs might be thinking. I tap Misty lightly on the shoulder—I'm too afraid of how she'll react if I grab her outright—and run for the ship's hatch.

"Crosskey. Do not let Crosskey escape," one of the hafelglob gurgles.

"What the hell is it talking about?" Misty hisses in my ear as our footsteps pound the concrete. We're almost to the hatch, but the hafelglob aren't too far behind. The hair on my arms rises, and I can almost feel their spongy, mucous-covered tentacles on the back of my neck. A *buzz-PEW* sound whizzes past my right ear and singes some of my split ends. Maybe they're instructed to capture me, but maybe it doesn't matter if I'm conscious or not.

Misty ducks under the wing of the craft and leaps nimbly into the hatch. She gasps for breath, and a large fireball erupts from her palm. There's a wet explosion to my right. I cover my face to avoid getting more of that mucous on me.

"If you're coming, you better get on," Misty yells, shooting an ice pellet over my left shoulder.

She doesn't help me. I jump and crawl on my stomach and roll safely inside as the hatch door snaps shut beside my ankles. Something splatters on the outside, and I try not to think about it.

Wil leans over the console, his fingers madly pressing buttons and flipping switches. "Jia, you ready?"

Jia sits with her legs tucked beneath her, her head slumped. She'd look defeated if her right hand wasn't balled into a fist, determined to fight. The other hand curls around the steel grating that serves as part of the floor, hiding whatever alien engine technology is below. She answers without looking up. "Yes, let's go."

I stand up just as the shuttle lurches. My heel catches in the steel grating and I slam backwards into the shuttle wall. I groan but my grievance can barely be heard over the overwhelming roar of the engine. My stomach feels queasy as we ascend. Slowly at first, then more rapidly. Jia and Misty and Wil are screaming at each other over the roar of the engines. Misty runs to the back of the hatch—three long strides is all it takes, the shuttle is so small—and opens it a crack and shoots a blast of ice. I catch a glimpse of the outside and see the blobs slithering towards three or four other dormant shuttles in the bay, half-covered with white sheets of their own.

My stomach turns again as the air becomes fluid like a watercolour. Jia is deep in a meditative state, but beads of sweat run down her pale forehead. She is the cloaking device for this shuttlecraft. I pray to whatever is listening that she has enough strength to keep us from harm, at least until we get to the mother ship.

Oh God. We are going to a mother ship, in *space*.

I run to the view screen in front of Wil. It's long and narrow, and I peer up at the ceiling of the bay. It's a giant hatch, and it's not opening, and we're rising fast.

"Wil . . . "

"I know, I'm on it!" he shouts.

He flattens his palm against the top of the shuttle easily, since the top of his head grazes the ceiling, and stares intensely out the view screen. The shuttle rocks violently as something larger than a laser gun fires at us off the starboard side. Our cloak wavers. Misty curses something and shuts the hatch, but not before firing one last blast at one of the other shuttles, which is gearing up to take off.

"It's opening . . . slowly . . . " Wil mutters some more under his breath, though I think he's cursing more than smooth talking the alien technology. "Jia, we need that cloak!"

Jia leans forward and presses her sweat-covered forehead to the floor. I rush to her side. Her ability to make things invisible relies on her ability to stay calm. I can't throw fire from my hands or open locks with a whisper, but I can help Jia remain grounded.

"Jia, talk to me," I say, all in one breath. "Tell me . . . tell me why you're here."

The ship rocks again. Jia falls to her side like an infant just learning to walk. I take note of the blood coming out of her nose and rest her head on my lap. "Think about something, something calm. Tell me about it."

Jia's face is scrunched up. She's thinking hard about something. "The lake."

"What about it?" I ask quickly.

"We were playing there. Me and my sister were swimming . . . " A smile breaks out over her distraught, wet face, and her eyes are moving beneath her lids. "And the water was actually warm for once. She was swimming towards me . . . " The smile disappears.

"What? Jia, what's wrong?" I ask.

Tears line Jia's eyes and escape, mingling with her sweat. "My sister . . . "

The wavering invisibility effect dissipates. We're visible again.

"Jia!" Misty shouts. She shoots me a deadly stare that says *you're not helping*.

Wil is frantic, running from console to console. "Ceiling bay door is opening, but I can't avoid their fire for long if we're not cloaked!"

"Don't think about your sister right now. She's fine. She's safe," I say, squeezing Jia's shoulders.

Jia shakes her head. "Not if she's accepted to Sparkstone."

The ship rocks again, and something in the console sparks and hits Wil in the face. His glasses go flying to the floor, and the ship begins to spiral.

"Jia!" I hug her close to me and think every happy thought I have—my love for my parents, the music I create, Ethan. "You can do this. We won't let them take your sister. Focus on the little girl in the lake, and your happy times with her. She's still with you."

My stomach reels as we tumble to our possible death. There's no time to think. One moment I'm holding on to Jia and about to vomit, the next, we're bathed in thick air, suspended in a watercolour paradise by her good thoughts and shaky inner calm.

Wil slides his glasses back on his face and hunches over the console again. The right side of his forehead looks burnt, but he seems fine. "Taking us up."

And then we're ascending again. Wil pilots the ship through the open bay door, and through the narrow view screen, I watch us tower over Sparkstone—first the university, then the town. My ears pop. The mountains— so beautiful in the distance with their mysterious insurmountable peaks—are white and grey dots on endless brown and green prairies.

Misty hurries to Wil's side at the console. "Are they—?"

"Still following, but I don't think they can see us. I hope." He throws a glance at me and Jia. "How is she now?"

Jia's breaths are staggered, and her face is the epitome of concentration. I squeeze her arms one last time and slip away from her. She doesn't react.

"I'll keep an eye on her," I say.

"Try not to get us killed," Misty spits.

I roll my eyes, and even though I want to make a witty remark of my own, I bite my tongue. We have less than an hour before Sparkstone goes up in flames, and who knows what could distract Jia. I'm not going to be responsible for our deaths. Misty's gaze is fiery but she backs down and settles herself by the hatch door.

Although the interior of the shuttle was not made for humans, it is roomy enough for the four of us. Three silver discs are embedded into the floor on the right side of the craft, and there are four thin black storage lockers on the left. I open them easily, but they're empty.

The engine—at least that's what I assume is making all the racket—quiets the higher we ascend. The night sky is a gradient of deep navies blanketed with stars fading into a more profound, endless black. I back away from the view screen. Looking through it is unsettling. I don't want to think about how high up I am, how Earth is getting smaller and smaller and we are going into the unknown vastness of space in the tiniest vehicle, made of only steel or whatever alien metal equates to steel. I didn't know it was possible to feel claustrophobic in a wide open space, but here I am.

I am in space.

This is not how I imagined my first space journey. I'm supposed to be one of those rich space tourists who goes to the space station, or maybe a famous concert pianist who is the first musician to play for thousands of people in space. Then afterward, I do some flips in a space suit at the opening for the world's first-ever outer-space shopping centre.

Which reminds me.

"Wil! Is there anti-gravity—?"

I'm falling upward before I can even finish the question. Now I understand why Jia is holding the grating—she has to be holding on to the craft it to remain invisible. My body panics. I think I'm falling, so I reach out to brace myself but end up flailing all over the place like a fool. Something grips the back of my shirt—it's Misty. She's dangling off a railing running close to the ceiling. I steady myself as she pulls me slowly, carefully, towards the railing.

"Thanks," I say.

Misty grunts.

"You don't have to thank her," Wil says. He's gripping a bar that runs along the edge of the console. "She doesn't believe in thank-yous."

"Niceties are a waste of time," she mutters.

Wil taps on the console, whispers something to the machine, and one of the three monitors above the view screen—previously abuzz with MS-DOS-like alien symbols—shows a crisp HD picture of Earth. There are four shuttlecrafts identical to the one we're in, but they're getting smaller by the second.

"Bad news is that the anti-grav is broken. Thought I had it fixed for a sec there, but the system was on its last legs anyway. I guess the Collective was storing these shuttles for repair," Wil says. He gestures to the monitor. "Good news is that the hafelglob look like they're breaking off pursuit. For now."

My gaze slides to Jia. Her thin black hair is streaked with sweat, and a droplet of blood leaves her nose and floats in the air.

"How much longer until we get to the mother ship?" I ask. "Assuming . . . we know where the mother ship is, right?"

Wil mutters more technobabble and then sighs. "Yes. It's in high orbit. Autopilot should take us the rest of the way. Only a couple of minutes. How are you doing, Jia?"

Jia lets out a short, high-pitched whine.

"It's okay, Jia. We'll be there soon," I say.

Clare C. Marshall

The closer we get to the mother ship, the more I feel as though we're merging onto the universe's largest highway. Shuttles like ours fly in orderly lines to and from the mother ship. Wil manoeuvres us so we are flying side by side with the other shuttles, undetected by the busy alien drivers around us.

I clear my throat and take a deep breath. We have less than an hour to make this work. My knuckles are pale from hanging on to the railing. "I think it's time you told me why a group of aliens is controlling a small university town for smart people in the Great White North."

I wait for a smart-alecky comment from Misty, but she just purses her lips.

Wil presses a few buttons with his free hand and lets us go on autopilot for a few minutes. He talks as if he's been rehearsing this speech for a little while. "We think the Collective is looking for people like us—people who can do things regular humans can't. Everyone at Sparkstone is wicked smart and that may have something to do with it. But we don't know why exactly they're here and . . . Sunni's dreams are all we have. They warned us what was going to happen next. She told us about you, that you have exactly what the Collective is looking for. Their genetic key to . . . whatever their endgame is." Wil smirks. "I hacked into their mainframe once. Was only in there for a few seconds before I was noticed, but what we learned, it was enough to let us know that Sparkstone is no ordinary university. Or town."

Misty scuffs her boots across the grated floor. "We don't know why they're here, but it can't be good. Handpickin' the brightest students from around the world? Probably lookin' to breed us or something." It's the first time I've seen Misty look truly uncomfortable.

"If you've known about this for months," I say, "why not try to escape? Why not take this shuttle and go somewhere, anywhere? To warn the military or the police or someone who can help?"

"We don't know if we can trust anyone. We don't know the Collective's true reach. Anyone could be an alien. And I wouldn't be able to keep an eye on them if I wasn't here," Wil replies. "We could be the only thing standing between the Collective and the human race becoming the next generation of lab rats."

My stomach is in knots. *I came to university to potentially learn how to be a scientist, not to become a rat.*

"And who would watch over the other people like us if we left?" Misty adds, folding her arms. "They could harvest their genes any day. We have to protect them."

I'm surprised by Misty's passion, even though I really shouldn't be. She's been nothing but angry the entire short period I've known her. Maybe she really does care about Sparkstone's students after all.

"I think I need to write all this down."

"You never write anything down. That's rule number one," Wil says. He taps his head. "Keep it in here. We're not just here because we have special powers. We're here because of our brains. Our intelligence."

I think back to the journal in Sunni's room, under her pillow. There was stuff in there, definitely alien stuff. Sunni broke rule number one—maybe that's how the Collective caught on to her special powers. The words are on the tip of my tongue, but something deep inside bars me from speaking. If Sunni is breaking her friends' rule, there must be a good reason.

"Sunni . . . mentioned something. When I was in her room. About Gene 213."

Wil only reads energy, I remind myself as the lie slips from my lips and into the world. I keep Sunni's image in my mind: her cheery face, her cute laugh. The memory of the conversation we had in her bedroom plays before my mind's eye. Wil studies me momentarily, as if also watching this mental memory, and then shoves his hands back in his pockets.

"Yeah," he says finally. "It's a gene, exists in five percent of the population. We think it's part of the reason why we have powers."

"But not everyone here has superpowers," I say.

"That we know of," Misty says, twirling a fireball in her left palm. Despite the gravity, the flame remains centred in her hand.

"But we're pretty sure that every student at the school has Gene 213." Wil adjusts his glasses. "Remember the blood test in the door? That's got to be how they confirm we have the gene."

"Yeah, but why go to the trouble of handpicking students from all over the world if they're not completely sure the students have the gene?"

"'Cause it's the gene that makes us smart, dumbass. Super smart, accomplished people are always on their radar. They'd rather pick up a couple of duds than risk *not* pickin' up someone they could use," Misty mumbles. The fireball in her hand cackles and glows fiercely. "They got people all over the place. For all we know, every famous university has got their Jadores and pimple-blobs suckin' up human brains and harvestin' the gene for their own sick experiments."

"Harvesting . . . our brains?" I grip the railing more tightly and pull myself against the wall.

"Not literally," Wil says, casting a disapproving glance at Misty. "Just the gene itself. In large concentrations."

"With all their technology . . . all that they can do . . . they can't just make this gene? They have to resort to taking it from *us*?"

"We're just stupid apes to them," Misty says. "Experiments. Walking meatbags with numbers stapled to our foreheads. Now we're moving targets. We're probably going to die in the next couple of days."

"We have less than forty-five minutes to rescue Sunni and save Sparkstone," Wil says, pulling himself back to the console and tapping more keys. "We should focus on that."

The mother ship looks like a larger version of the shuttle we're flying, and far more intimidating. The hull is a venomous, smoky green, and streaks of silver run from the tip of the starboard side down to the edge of what I can only describe as a large fin on the ship's underbelly. Pinpricks of light flicker on and off in orderly rows on every deck. Windows. Each one of those lights probably represents an alien, and there's a whole galaxy of lights scattered across the hull. A whole city, floating above our heads, and we didn't even know it. I count six different docking bays where ships scurry in and out in orderly lines and my stomach sinks.

We're doomed. Even with the tune on repeat in my head, and Wil's ability to sense people, the ship is too big. We're never going to find Sunni and stop Sparkstone from blowing to smithereens.

But I say nothing. There's no going back now.

I'm afraid we're not going to fit inside the docking bay. *Some alarm will sound,* I think as we inch closer and hug the craft next to us. But the bay door is at least three times as wide as the shuttles and we pass through easily. Hundreds of shuttles are docked in rows that stretch into the darkness. The shuttles float in the bay, attached at the hatch to pressurized doors. Wil glides through the rows until he finds an empty spot far away from the rest of the shuttles, and starts docking procedures.

"Gravity coming online."

I make sure I'm bracing the wall next to the lockers this time as the gravity stabilizes. The floor sucks me down and I'm a thousand pounds again. I check my phone. Thirty minutes left.

Wil is communing with the alien console. "All right. It looks like the hafelglob on the surface have sent a bunch of warnings to the mother ship about our arrival. The word on the street"—he twirls a finger in the air—"is that they're trying to shut down all inbound and outbound traffic. But this is the only outpost for . . . whoa. This is the only outpost in this solar system." Wil shoots us a glance. "There are hundreds of thousands of aliens on this ship, and they need supplies. And the ships here have to refuel before going to . . . well . . . there are at least eight planet or station names in languages I can barely pronounce. Whoever is in charge of shutting down stuff on board, they are *not* happy that there might be intruders. Lucky for us, they also seem to think that four humans aren't going to be a problem."

I purse my lips. *The moment we step onto that ship, they're going to be looking for us. And considering the technology we've seen so far, they will have no problems finding us.*

"And . . . " Wil taps a few more buttons and then dusts his hands off. "Done. I've forged some communication about us coming from the surface for a refuel and personnel change. Hopefully that will be enough to keep us going for a while. Always wanted to fly one of these things. Hopefully we can fly her home, too." He looks mournfully at Jia. "You're done, Jia. We're proud of you."

Jia gasps for air and the world returns to its normal colours. She collapses on the ground and I kneel beside her.

"I'm all right," she says weakly. "I just need . . . a few minutes."

We all need a few minutes. But time is ticking. "We need a plan," I say.

"There's got to be some weapons in this damn . . . " Misty trails off as she throws open one of the locker doors, and it slams against the adjacent locker. Something rattles on one of the shelves. She reaches in and removes a thick silver band about twice as long as my middle finger. She examines it with disgust. "What's this? Alien jewellery? No thanks."

I could have sworn there was nothing in there when I

checked before. Misty's about to throw the band on the floor when I step in. "Can I see it?"

She shrugs and practically throws the thing at me. To my surprise, the gleaming steel is warm, not cool, to the touch. Six blue buttons, no bigger than my fingertip, line the band in pairs of three around a large silver knob. It looks familiar, and I place it almost immediately: the hafelglob were wearing these in Sunni's room.

Misty's rooting through the shelves but only uncovers a fistful of bands. Three more, to be exact. "Just more jewellery."

"May I?" Wil asks, and I hand mine to him.

Jia gets up off the floor. Even though it's only been a minute or two, she's regained some colour in her porcelain cheeks. Her exhaustion shows only in the lines beneath her eyes, and nowhere else. She smiles at me wearily as she examines the shuttle. Her eyes rest on the three silver discs. "The silver on the floor looks similar to the silver in those bands."

"Hmm?" Wil looks up from the band and casts a quick eye at the discs. "Yes, the ship told me those are teleportation pads."

"Teleportation pads!" Misty expostulates. "Why didn't we just—?"

"Non-operational," Wil cuts in. "But these bands . . . I feel like these might do something."

"The hafelglob were wearing them," I say quietly.

Maybe I didn't look thoroughly enough when I searched the locker. But I don't remember hearing any rattling in the lockers when the gravity went offline and came back on either. Unease settles within me.

"They're similar," Wil agrees, turning it over, and raising a thick eyebrow. "These ones feel more . . . "

He presses a blue button to the left of the shiny silver knob and the bracelet snaps around his wrist. Jia and I jump back in surprise. Wil laughs nervously and mutters to it as he tries to communicate with the alien technology.

His muttering becomes more worried when he pulls at the band.

"It's stuck," he says. "And none of these buttons—"

Suddenly, the band flashes blue and a gel-like, dark blue liquid spreads up his arm, over his face, and down around the rest of his body. Jia shouts his name in panic, but Wil holds up a hand. When the gel settles, it's tightly fitted around his skin and clothes like full-body wet suit. Only his eyes and mouth are unprotected. He looks as if he's about to rob a bank that's located at the bottom of the ocean.

I'm trying not to laugh, but it bursts out of me anyway. We're in space, Sunni's been captured, the university is being run by aliens and is about to explode, and something has decided that one-piece body suits are going to protect us.

"Yeah. I know. They're crazy looking," Wil says. "But I always thought it would be neat for us to have uniforms." He checks himself out. "You guys should put one of these on. It's harmless. Designed to interface with your biochemistry and create a suit that is environment resistant. I bet we can control it, so it doesn't go all over our bodies."

"Yeah, I'm not putting one of those things on," Misty says, crossing her arms. "In case you've forgotten, which clearly you have, we're here to save Sunni."

"And if we run into any of our professors up here, and they recognize us, they'll 'transfer' us to a different school," Wil replies. "Then everyone will die."

I look at my phone. Twenty-five minutes until Sparkstone explodes.

Wil tosses the armbands at us. I hate the idea of anything alien touching me after everything I've seen in the past twelve hours—and I hate even more that I didn't see them in the lockers in the first place—but I also don't want my face to be posted on every alien wanted poster on Earth, and in space. I awkwardly catch the armband and stumble back as it slams into my chest. My hand hovers over it. Misty and Jia are watching me, as if waiting for me to make the mistake that they want to avoid.

"Well? Put it on," Wil says.

I gulp. We are losing precious minutes and I have to be brave.

I clasp the armband around my left wrist and it snaps shut, hugging my skin tightly. I think about the creatures from the *Alien* movie briefly as the hair on my arm stands upright. Where the ends meet is almost invisible to the naked eye. Whatever this alien technology is, it doesn't look as if it's coming off any time soon. Wearily, Jia follows my lead, and Misty stubbornly latches hers with a reluctant click.

"What button did you press?" I ask.

Wil cranes his neck and points a gel-covered finger to the blue button directly to the left of the silver knob. "That one." He looks at Jia. "I hope you'll be able to use your invisibility with it on."

"You mean there's not a button for that already?" Misty says dryly.

"I dunno. Why don't you try and find out?"

Misty's response is an icy glare.

"I will try," Jia says.

"If not, we'll just be extra careful," Wil says.

The weight of my finger presses down on the blue button and a cool, tingling sensation erupts from the armband. Liquid expands from the band and spreads over my arm. It feels as if someone is covering me in sticky plastic wrap, and I start to regret ever getting into this as the alien goo covers most of my body. Misty squeezes her eyes shut, and her hands are ablaze. Jia looks as if she's meditating again as her form is enrobed by the gel.

Soon my whole body—except my mouth and my eyes—is covered, and the gel settles as it did on Wil. I stretch. My new alien-goo suit stretches with it. It's as though I'm not even wearing clothes underneath, as though the skirt I'm wearing has dissolved into my skin. A full-body suit. I'm like cat woman, without the claws. *Or the boots.* I sulk as I stare at my feet. They're covered too. I feel for my hair; the gel has pressed it tightly against my back, though it doesn't tickle or hurt. I'm a little concerned, but there are definitely bigger things to worry about.

The four of us look almost identical now—aside from our varying heights and body weights. Jia flickers between visibility and invisibility. "This gel suit will work."

Misty flexes and lights up the spacecraft with a ball of fire. "Works with my flames too."

I should be trying out my superpowers but I don't have any, and I'd make a joke about it but my hand is hovering over where my pocket should be, thinking about the time on my cell phone. The repeating tune whistles more intensely than it did twenty minutes ago. Wil's right. The source is on board the mother ship.

Wil strides to the hatch to my left and places a deft hand on it, concentrating. A moment later it whirs open, revealing a narrow corridor with grated flooring, a ton of blinking panels, and another set of thicker metal doors with another blinking panel.

Great. Security.

"Wait," Jia says as Wil starts to step out. "We have to stick together."

"There's no one on the other side," Wil replies, but he spins and takes Jia's outstretched hand.

Jia's eyes are sympathetic as she extends a hand to me. "Are you all right?"

I can barely believe that she's asking me how I feel, after she just carried us all to safety, through space.

"Yeah." I sound more confident than I feel. *We're in space, in alien space suits. No big deal.*

Misty's right hand is smouldering hot when she grabs my arm. The suit seems to dull the heat somewhat, but I'm not sure how useful it will be in combat.

Jia takes my hand and my stomach drops as we flicker into her watery, invisible world once again. Wil leads the way into the grated, narrow corridor between the shuttlecraft and the ship. Lights blink and flash at us and I search the ceiling for cameras. *Not that I would know what an alien camera looks like. Then again, maybe I do know.* Black olive circles line the ceiling, and I pray that Jia's invisibility will buy us some time before we're discovered.

Wil fingers the control panel to the right of the door and mutters under his breath. The longer I stand on the grating, the more aware I become of the enclosed space, the tightness of Misty's grip on my right arm, and the weight of my cell phone in my gelled-over pocket.

Dread and surprise twists my stomach as a loud buzz fills the air and the large doors hiss open, revealing a metal wall and a narrow corridor running perpendicular to us. The four of us trudge as quietly as four people can trudge off the grated floor and onto the alien mother ship.

We're on an alien mother ship. My inner nerd is geeking out, hard.

Do you know which way to the detonator? Wil asks telepathically.

I look left, and then right. My movement is slow, as if I'm swooshing my limbs underwater. The gravity feels heavier here. The tune is everywhere but it's tugging on my body. As if it wants me to find it. I nod my head to the right, and whisper, "This way."

I gasp when the door to the loading corridor hisses shut again. Jia shoots me a silencing glare.

"And Sunni? Which way is she?" Misty asks Wil.

Wil gives her a stern look. *We're not splitting up. We have to think about the thousands of people in Sparkstone. Sunni wouldn't want us to put her before the town.*

"The TOWN is full of ALIENS!" Misty hisses.

I remember Sunni's words: *I am already lost.* "But there are innocent people down there too," I point out.

Misty snarls at me. "I *wasn't* talking to you."

"We should be quiet," Jia says, but her voice is almost a whisper and it's hard to hear her over my racing heart and Misty's fingernails clicking against the metal wall.

"Do you know where she is?" Misty hisses.

Wil rubs his temple. He looks weary. Jia looks as though she's going to be sick. Only Misty maintains a fierce persistence and doesn't show weakness—maybe it's this persistence that makes Jia and Wil more tired.

"This way," Wil whispers, pointing upward.

"Great. Now I just have to learn to teleport," Misty snaps.

"I can only make you invisible, I can't make your voices silent," Jia says.

Misty's grip on me tightens. "No one has to talk, just point the way and help me figure out how to get there."

I look down the hallway behind us for hafelglob and almost cry out when I see someone else instead. He looks about forty, but his smile is youthful and full of mischief. He's looking straight at me, even though I'm holding Jia's hand and invisible. I clench my teeth. His flat blond-grey curls shimmer in and out of reality like heat waves in the middle of the desert, and the laugh lines and age wrinkles that crease his face deepen, disappear, and reappear again, as if in a looping time-lapse video.

I know this man. With every fibre of my being I know him, and the déjà vu is so strong. It's not just because his image was in Sunni's dream journal. No, how I know him is deep in my subconscious, wedged in so deeply that I'm afraid it's etched onto my brain tissue and all the way down my throat to my stomach. I feel like vomiting.

He's curling a finger at me. Beckoning me closer.

I draw a sharp breath. "We should go this way instead," I whisper, pointing towards the man.

Misty and Wil stop arguing. I only glance at them for a moment, and in that split second, the mysterious man disappears.

"Why?" Misty demands.

Is the music louder that way? Wil asks. *Because my sense is telling me that the bridge is more to this side of the ship.* He waves to the right, to the place where the music is whispering for me to go.

Ugh! How do I explain to my multitalented, newfound friends that I am not only a music player stuck on repeat but also a hallucinating madwoman?

"Yes. Well, it seems to have changed direction," I say.

Wil furrows his brow but seems to accept my flimsy reasoning. This is the second time I've lied to him today. I pray it's worth it.

I take the lead, then Misty, Wil, and Jia. This corridor bends a few feet down from the loading bay door and then continues in a straight line for what seems like forever. This must not be a heavily trafficked part of the ship, or maybe everyone is working or enjoying their alien lives right now, because we run into no one. I hope I'm going the right way. The music, once so clear, seems to be coming from multiple directions. Deciding to follow some guy in blind faith, who doesn't exist, was not a good idea. The minutes are slipping away with each step we take.

We're never going to find Sunni. We're never going to save Sparkstone. The negative thoughts invade my mind until I almost believe them.

There are signs on the grey alien steel walls next to a few of the doors, but they're in some symbol language. I recall Misty's major: languages. "Misty. Can you read that?"

She turns her fiery gaze on me and then on the alien signage. If only her looks could burn holes in walls instead of her hands, then maybe we would get somewhere.

"Does it *look* like I speak effin alien?"

Wil comes to my defence. *You speak seven other languages, and you can read in several others, so it's only logical to conclude—*

She rips her hand from Wil's grasp, rendering us visible. "Oh, what, so you're a computer now?"

"Let's just keep going, okay?" I whisper. "Down this—"

"Hey, guys. HEY!"

That's when I realize we're *all* visible.

Jia's scream echoes through the hall and my heart freezes. How did she get over there? Behind her is an alien that looks like a human-sized catfish, and it's holding a large weapon to the side of her neck. Two more run around a corner ahead of me, carrying identical guns, and skid to a stop a few feet away. The guns light up and beep as the ammo clicks into place. The wide barrel points a laser straight at the middle of my chest.

CHAPTER 9

"Jia!" Misty hisses.

"I told you. I can't hide *voices*."

The aliens open their fish-like mouths and start clicking their long, thin tongues.

"I think they want us to go with them," I say, raising my hands.

"Take me to Sunni," Misty demands. She repeats this in several languages: French, Spanish, Japanese, and a few others that I don't immediately recognize. The aliens continue to click and hiss the same tones. One shoves the nozzle of the gun between my eyes. His long fingernail looks as if it's about to apply pressure to the trigger.

"I think we should just do as they say and see what happens," I repeat. "Because I really don't want to die on a spaceship. Wil, is there any way to communicate that we're not here to hurt them, that we just want to see Sunni?"

"Already trying. Not sure if their brains are receptive to complex messages."

I lift my arms higher in the air. If I've learned anything from my favourite science fiction shows, it's that surrendering doesn't mean the end of the story. It usually means the protagonist actually gets to live and discover what the baddies are up to. I pray that Sunni is still alive and maybe, somehow, we can get out of this in one piece.

The aliens are clicking again, and the one with Jia prods her with its gun, forcing her to move forward. I reach for her hand as she passes and squeeze it tightly. There is fear in her eyes, and her palms are sweaty, but she smiles at me in gratitude. *Together, we can get through this,* I want to say. I don't know why I'm so hopeful, since I have zero experience in being a hostage on an alien spaceship, but I have to believe that the countless hours I've spent reading and watching science fiction is going to help keep us alive somehow.

Misty spits on the grated floor at the aliens' feet. "Fine. I'll go with you. But that doesn't mean I surrender. You got that? You shoot us, you'll be a pile of stinkin' ash on the floor before you can even think about calling for backup. Wil, you think you can translate that?"

The aliens' guns light up and whir as they point at Misty. These snarling fishmen are clicking like typewriters in overdrive and do not look happy about Misty's objection to being their prisoner.

Wil closes his eyes and concentrates, and then I can hear him in my mind. *We mean you no harm. We just want to see our friend.*

And then I see a million pictures of Sunni, a slideshow going too quickly. Sunni laughing, Sunni eating in a place that's not the Sparkstone cafeteria, Sunni and Misty giggling at something on a computer screen, Sunni speaking in tutorial. Sunni twirling, dancing by herself. They click, click, click through my brain in time with the bomb tune. The fishmen's long, dangly barbels jiggle as their heads shake. Their wet eyes blink with a squishy sound as they process the images invading their minds.

The fishmen regroup around us, squishing against our gel suits as if we're a bunch of packed sardines, and half lead, half push us down the hallway. *This is where the man wanted us to go in the first place,* I think as we pass sliding doors and grey steel panels. *Did he mean for us to be captured too?*

I can't reach for my cell phone through my gel suit without being seen or caught. But we've got at least fifteen minutes until Sparkstone's destruction.

We're taken to a large circular deck. The back walls are glass so clear that it can't possibly exist, and the view steals my breath. Earth is so close, a giant ball of blue and green in the middle of endless darkness. I almost bump into the fishman guard behind me, and he shoves me forward. I shield my eyes from the glare of the sun as we trudge across the grated floor. Through the crisscross of the grating, I see a multitude of alien bodies manning computer stations and panels. I can only assume we're on the bridge of the mother ship. I want to lie down and take in the moment but my focus is captured by two figures standing on a platform in front of the impossibly tall observation windows.

Sunni. She's alive, at least. She's sitting with her legs beneath her with her eyes closed—as if she's meditating. When the fishmen guide us towards the platform, Sunni seems to become aware of our presence and stands. She doesn't jump for joy that we're here. She doesn't scream *help me* or otherwise indicate that she needs us to save her. There's a sadness in her face that transcends words. Deep lines crease her forehead. I don't remember them being there this morning. Some of them look like cuts. Her lips tremble slightly, like a dam buckling, struggling to hold back the weight of the water behind it.

A tall, thick-chested woman casts a shadow over Sunni. Tiny green scales cover the woman's body, but unlike the fishmen, she has a humanoid face—full black lips, an upturned nose, and even a semblance of black hair that's been shaved in a tight buzz cut against the scaly skin on her scalp. Where her ears should be are fleshy, scaly knobs and waving slits that I guess might be gills. The top half of her curvy body is highlighted with strips of fabric that cover and lift her breasts and connect to a black belt around her waist. The wide slits in her long skirt that descends from her belt expose her long, muscular legs. I could be imagining things, but the glint from the overhanging lights seems to reveal tiny black hairs beneath the scales.

It's her eyes that draw me in. Merciless black holes that reflect a world of chaos and destruction, dead like a deer's in that they lack emotion but alive with a horrible intelligence that relishes the idea of telling me what my next move will me. And as I stare into those black orbs that serve as eyes, I know without a doubt whom I'm facing.

"So. You have been caught, *humans*." Jadore spits at our race name in disgust, but she also looks confused. "The scent of humans is all over you. Unless . . . " She squeezes her long scaly fingers into fists. "Are you footmen from the council, sent to oppose me? Please. This specimen"—she points to Sunni—"has uncovered confidential information about the Collective and must be processed earlier than the other participants."

I look over to Wil and Misty. Of the four of us, they're the two who I think will say *something* to keep up our deceit. But their lips are tight, thin lines.

"Tell me who sent you," Jadore warns. She takes a cautious step forward as her black orbs dart around the room. "Campbell, is this one of your tricks? The Collective forbids you from using your talents this way."

Campbell, as in Joseph G. Campbell? Even thinking the name gives me chills. I wonder if he's an alien too.

I wonder if he's the man I saw earlier. I remember the initials beneath Sunni's hastily drawn portrait of him: J.G.C. *Maybe, just maybe . . .*

Wil's voice is a thundering hum in my head, deep and commanding. *We are the Sparks. You will release the girl and deliver her to us, or suffer the consequences.*

"The Sparks?" Jadore sounds unconvinced. Our chance of survival is dying with each nanosecond as Jadore casts a thorough, suspicious gaze upon the four of us. "Tell me who you really are, or I'll have you terminated."

The alien guards close in on us. I flinch but I don't dare make any other movements.

Release the girl, Wil repeats. His hands are balled into fists at his side. I mirror him.

Jadore's heels click on the hard floor as she steps off the platform. I secretly hope they will catch on the grating, but her green toes and painted purple toenails stop just before the change in the floor.

"You will not tell me what to do on *my* ship," she declares.

Prompted by a flick of Jadore's scaly finger, the alien guards spring into action. One grabs Misty and is thrown across the room. Steam courses off his charred body, which is a disgusting mess of cooked fish meat and plastic. Another goes for Jia, but she grabs Wil and the two of them are out of sight and reach within milliseconds. Which leaves me defenceless. Rough hands clasp my shoulders and yank me off the ground. My feet are dangling in the air. Misty's busy fighting off the other two alien guards and I'm afraid to scream, in case Jadore recognizes my voice.

"You sure that you want the girl?" Jadore reaches into her belt and pulls out what looks like a pen. It's beeping, and a red light blinks in time. The tune playing in the back of my mind intensifies and shoves its way into my ears. I bite down on my lip hard to keep from crying out. Jadore holds the detonator—the fate of Sparkstone and thousands of innocent lives—in her green, scaly hand.

"Five minutes," Jadore says, "and everything on Sparkstone campus goes up in flames."

The fishmen guards release me, and they stop fighting Misty and the others. Everyone is frozen in a single moment, staring at Jadore and her blinking detonator. But Jadore's gaze falls between Misty and me, waiting for us to react.

And in that moment, I realize why we're here.

This isn't about saving people at Sparkstone from a bomb threat.

It's not even really about Sunni.

It's about us.

Jadore wanted to see who would come for Sunni if she were in trouble. And she's willing to put everything the Collective has worked for on the line in order to expose the people the Collective needs the most—those with active Gene 213 inside them. Sunni is the bait. The bombs are the grave danger that threaten innocent lives.

But that's not the worst of it.

Sunni's face is a mask of calm. She *knew* this was going to happen. And yet, she didn't even tell her best friends. Why?

Wil speaks for us again. *If the Collective is willing to sacrifice thousands of potential Gene 213 carriers, that is their prerogative.*

This is not the response Jadore was hoping for. Her thumb flicks open the top of the detonator, revealing a small black button. The tune that the bomb sings blares full force in my mind, and I grit my teeth in agony.

"My prerogative," Jadore hisses, "is the glory of the Harvest, and the glory of being the future face of the Collective."

Her sharp nails gleam as she brings down her thumb. The music burns my ears and somehow I know that the moment she hits that button, not only will everything at Sparkstone explode, but my eardrums will shatter as well. I will not be a deaf musician, I can't.

My hand slides through the gel suit, into my skirt pocket, and clasps the only thing I have—my cell phone. I thrust it at Jadore. I've never been good at sports, but on this night, my aim is true. The cell phone bounces off the side of her green scaly head, crashes to the floor, and slides across the black tile. Caught off guard, Jadore hisses violently.

"Then you have made your *choice*," she says.

Cackling electricity and the smell of burnt plastic fills the air as Jadore raises her palm towards Sunni. Misty is readying a fireball the size of her head but she is not fast enough. White-hot twisted lightning shoots from Jadore's palm and envelops Sunni's frail form. Sunni screams in agony and crumbles to the floor at Jadore's feet. Her body twitches involuntarily and her blonde curls cover her face.

Jadore's black, reflective orbs are steady on me.

"No . . . NO!" Misty's fireball dissolves in black smoke. She seems to forget Jadore and everyone else as she drops to her knees before Sunni's limp figure. Sparks bounce off Misty's gel suit as she gathers Sunni in her lap. She buries her head in Sunni's chest and pinches her arms for a reaction, then shakes her, screaming, "Come back! Don't you *dare* die . . . "

Sunni does not respond. Her chest is still.

My stomach clenches.

As she lays Sunni's body softly on the black tile, Misty narrows her angry eyes at me in an accusatory glare. Twin swirls of red and white-blue flare up from her palms, and I back away, afraid of my fate. But I'm not her target. Misty's power fires at Jadore. Jadore laughs as the flames lick her scaly skin, and she hits the metal band around her left wrist.

"Good luck saving yourselves, Sparks. You don't know *what* you are meddling with."

Jadore begins to dissolve. The band, a teleportation device! Jia and Wil close in on her, but just before Jadore disappears completely, she draws a laser gun from her belt and fires at the ceiling. I look up, and my mind reels with panic.

Dozens upon dozens of black boxes connected with coloured wires line the silver metal ceiling. Jadore's laser hits a large box above her head and sends a chain reaction rippling above our heads. An explosion rocks the ship and knocks us all to the floor. Alarms blare warnings in an alien language.

"NO!" Misty roars.

I scramble to my feet. Sweat pools on my forehead from the electrical fire bearing down on us from the ceiling. It's spreading down the walls. This is not the worst of it. Jadore, her fishmen lackies, and the alien personnel who had been manning the stations beneath us are gone. And so is Sunni's body.

The music, once so loud and blended with my brain like a song stuck on repeat, is now silent. Did . . . did we stop the bomb from detonating?

"She's gone . . . " Misty stares with clenched fists out to the endless vacuum of space and out at our planet, floating in its lonely orbit.

"Do we know for sure that she's . . . ?" Jia doesn't want to say it. Fire cackles above us to fill her silence. Everything about this moment feels so final, as if we're on the verge of the end.

Wil looks uncomfortable. "I think so. I . . . I didn't *sense* . . . "

Misty shoots him a menacing glare, and his sentence ends. She's standing so close to the window, and I wonder how strong it is—I wonder if she could use her power to break the alien glass and suck us all into space. I take a step backwards.

Wil changes course, but he talks with a lump in his throat. "Jadore and the rest of them must have teleported out with their arm devices. I don't think ours do that." He steps onto the platform—careful to avoid Misty by the windows. He grabs the fallen detonator and wraps his gelled hands around it.

"I was going to stop her, before she hit the button," he says as he examines the alien device. His body stiffens. "This isn't a detonator. This . . . this isn't connected to anything."

I panic. "Then the boxes at the school, they were decoys? And the music . . . ?"

My questions are interrupted by a loud *bang* followed by a *crack* and a *BOOM*. The sound resonates through the bridge as part of the ceiling grating falls to the floor and hits one of the railings. It snaps, and together the pieces tumble to the consoles below. More warnings and another *BEEP BEEP* alarm sounds. A female voice in an alien language overpowers the other sounds and speaks in a calm, but direct manner.

"We have to get out of here," Misty says. "How do I get this thing off my face . . . ?" She hits the metal alien band around her wrist and the dark blue liquid recedes from her face and her hands. "This effin ship is going to detach."

"Detach?" Jia asks.

"I didn't effin stutter. Look, I'm not an engineer, but the effin voice on the effin com is sayin' somethin' about compromised control centres and evacuations and rerouting power to the auxiliary control. Okay?" She throws a haughty glance at Wil. "Which way to the shuttle?"

"How long until this part detaches?" Wil asks.

"And what about Sparkstone? All of the people down there?" I demand.

Another piece of the ceiling falls, but this time, a light show of exploding wires races above our heads like a comet. The control consoles below us spark, and the smell of burnt plastic grows exponentially stronger.

"Don't you get it?" Misty shouts. She grabs my arms and shakes me, sending burning hot flames up one arm and burning ice up another. "The bombs were a *ruse!* They just wanted to mess with us while they were abductin' Sunni."

I throw her off me. "But the music I heard was real."

"Yeah, and it's gone now. Thanks to you, Sunni is gone too." Her voice quakes a bit on the last part, but she powers through with her anger. "We have one minute to get back to the shuttles. Maybe two. She's already counting down."

The calm female voice is sprouting off short syllables in two-four time.

Wil thinks fast. "We don't have time to get back to the shuttles and take off. I think . . . I think the shuttle bay we were in was part of this section. We'd be floating dead in space before we got there." Before Misty can have an explosion of her own, Wil continues. "But those might be able to help."

He points over to the right wall. Three silver discs protrude from the floor, but unlike the teleporters on the shuttle, these ones have silver halos above them, about seven feet off the ground. Each halo is attached to a long flat pole on the wall. There's a beeping control panel sparking next to the teleporters.

Wil rushes to the panel and runs his hands over the buttons and screens. "It's functioning, but barely. There's enough backup power for one last teleport. I can set it to go in a few seconds. Everyone on the discs."

Misty and Jia stand together on one, and Wil hops on another. I move towards the third.

"INGRID!"

Jia screams my name, and I lunge for the teleportation platforms as one of the ceiling panels comes crashing down on my legs. I scream and try to wiggle free as the adjacent tile sparks and falls on my back. My chest slams against the floor. My breath is wheezy. I am pinned.

"Come on, Ingrid!"

Jia is about to move off the platform but Misty holds her back—for good reason. A large metal sheet from the ceiling collapses in a fiery, smoky blaze right in front of them.

"I've already locked in the teleportation coordinates!" Wil shouts. "Only thirty seconds!"

Misty looks worried. "And forty until the ship detaches."

"There . . . there must be a way . . . " I say.

The ship begins to rumble and tilt. Debris slides across the floor but the panels on top of me are heavy and barely shift at all. The weight of the panels just seems to increase, and one of them brushes against the alien band around my arm that controls the gel suit. It recedes from my arms and face and hands, exposing my skin to the elements. My cell phone drifts towards my desperate fingers. I grasp it as though it's a lifeline.

Wil is trying to concentrate, but he just keeps shaking his head. "I can't. The system keeps overriding me. There's nothing I can do."

I squeeze my eyes shut. I can't bear to look at them.

I came all this way to save the school, only to be fooled by an alien professor. And Sunni. Sunni, whose death could've been prevented—even though she didn't want to be saved. If I had only controlled my emotions . . .

Reach inside yourself.

The voice is not my own. It sounds . . . like Sunni's voice?

But how is that possible?

The ceiling panels rattle and something loud cracks and hisses above me. Alarms blaze in my ears and the Sparks' shouts meld into one. Thick smoke gathers and I can barely keep my eyes open. My lungs fill with the stuff and I'm deep in a coughing fit as the floor begins to burn beneath me.

"I can't hold this!" Wil cries. "Ingrid . . . "

I gaze out the tall windows into space. Earth. I long for home.

"Ingrid . . . " Jia's voice fades as she, Misty, and Wil dissolve into a blue haze on the platform.

So this is how I will go. In a fiery blaze in space.

Just as the ceiling panel gives way and falls, I turn my head and take in Earth's beauty one last time. Clutching my cell phone, I bring up Ethan's number and press the call button.

A sensation of swimming in thick air. I am sucked into a vacuum of darkness.

Then, nothing.

CHAPTER 10

The sunrise stabs my eyes. I shield them and consider going back to sleep, to whatever science-fiction-story dream I was having—the one where I'm fighting aliens with some newfound friends and crushing on an adorable British guy at a fantastical university in the middle of nowhere.

Then I remember. That was no dream.

I died in space just now.

I sit up quickly, and climb to my feet. The green, grassy plains stretch into the horizon. There's a grey outline out there, maybe some kind of gate. It's so far off and the sun is blinding me, so it's hard to tell. A brisk breeze whips my dark red hair around my shoulders and tickles my skin. I've never felt more alive.

So this is what heaven looks like.

Maybe Sunni is waiting to greet me.

The grass rustles behind me. "Rough night?"

The accent squeezes my nerves as I turn around slowly. "Ethan?"

What's he doing in heaven? Did he die last night, alone in his studio, with nothing but his art to comfort him?

He looks a little unkempt, as if he saw a sleepless night. Nonetheless, he smiles. There's a bit of charcoal on his forehead. Dead or alive, he's perfect.

"You all right there?" He reaches out and pulls a strand of grass from my hair as it blows around my face.

I'm too stunned to speak. His touch feels so real. Maybe I have one foot on Earth and another foot in the next realm, and this is my chance to say goodbye.

Say something. Anything.

"I was . . . I just woke up."

"I can see that." He looks amused. "Now I know one more thing about you, Ingrid."

That I can't keep my promises. That I died last night and I'm a ghost and you can see me and maybe you're a ghost too.

"What's that?"

"You can't hold your liquor."

A laugh escapes me and my face feels hot, even though I'm not facing the sun. "No . . . no that's not what happened. Ethan, I'm really sorry I couldn't come to your studio . . . "

"I got your text."

"I'm sorry. I really wanted to be one of your models. I really wanted to get to know you better. But I guess . . . I guess I'll never get a chance to do that." The morning sun is hot on the back of my neck. It's so hot that it must be real. I glance over my shoulder to look but it's so bright— it's the light at the end of the tunnel, calling me home. "This is goodbye, Ethan. But there's something that I want to do first, before I go."

Ethan looks perplexed but it doesn't matter. I wrap my arms around his shoulders and bring my lips to his. He smells like aftershave and charcoal and fresh paint, and I kiss him as though I'll never kiss anyone again, because I won't. He's kissing me back, pulling me closer to him. I just want to be as near to him as possible before I lose all sensation in the physical realm.

I peek and our noses touch. His eyes are filled with bewilderment but there's something else there too. I want to stay like this forever. I take in everything about the moment: the smell of the dewy grass, the feel of his skin, his hands on my waist, the cluster of brick buildings behind Ethan, the road. I never thought I'd feel sad to leave Sparkstone, and the new friends I made here.

Wait . . . Sparkstone?

"Um, you know Ingrid, I generally don't make out with girls I just met," Ethan says. "You must have really drunk a lot. Where did you go last night?"

I slowly pull away from him. The campus is real enough. Ethan is real enough. And . . . I feel real too. My hands are solid and they felt Ethan's warm skin with no difficulty.

Movement catches my eye. In the distance, I see a tall man waving at us. Wil.

Oh no. I'm not dead at all. I'm alive.

Somehow, I survived. I was really in space, and the silver metal band is clamped around my arm, and I'm still alive, and . . .

And I just made out with Ethan.

I take off. "I have to go."

"Ingrid, wait, I didn't mean—"

"Neither did—" But I don't finish. I did mean my kiss. I really, really, did. But I'm too embarrassed to face him. I thought I was dead and I poured my heart out to him.

He's going to think I'm a crazy person.

Ethan's talking again, but whatever he's saying, it's swallowed by the grassy plain as I run towards Wil. He looks at me as if I really am a ghost.

"You're alive," he says.

"I don't know how," I reply, shaking my head. "I just woke up in the field. Do you think that means that Sunni . . . ?"

Wil gives me a grave look. "Jadore took her. As far as I know, she's not coming back. But you. One minute, I couldn't sense you at all, and now, here you are. We have twenty minutes before tutorial starts, and we have a lot to talk about. C'mon."

I follow him towards the girls' dorms.

Why am I still alive? It isn't fair.

I think about the voice I heard just before the ceiling panel fell on me. I'm sure it was Sunni's voice, warning me. But maybe it was just my imagination.

We head towards Jia's dorm room in Rita House but before we can reach it, Wil and I run into Ms. Agailya.

"Ingrid! I have been looking for you all morning," she says with a warm smile. "I have good news. A room has opened up on the third floor. We are working on cleaning it out now, and one of my staff members will be speaking with you about customization options."

"Oh . . . that's great," I say. A sense of dread consumes my stomach. "If it's okay for me to ask, whose room was it before?"

Ms. Agailya looks uncomfortable. "Do you remember Sunni Harris? The girl you met when you arrived yesterday?"

Wil's voice drills into my mind. *We should go. Anything she says is going to be a lie.*

I know Wil's probably right, but I'm curious about what Ms. Agailya has to say. "What about Sunni?"

"I'm afraid she transferred early this morning. Nothing serious, but sometimes Sparkstone cannot offer its students everything they want."

My heart is ready to break. I have to remain calm. The way Ms. Agailya talks and acts, I have trouble believing that she's on the Collective's side. Even Jadore seemed to doubt her loyalty to the Collective. Everything about her is ethereal and radiant. I bite my tongue to focus on the pain, on something other than my anxiety regarding the alien attack yesterday.

"Drop by my office later, Ingrid, and we will discuss your major and new dorm room," she says. "You two should be getting to tutorial. Professor Jadore is running early today and expects her students to conform to her standards and sense of time."

I'm anxious to talk with Jia and Misty about what happened last night, and I'm especially anxious to talk about Sunni's fate, but it seems as though that will have to wait. As Ms. Agailya passes us, her fingertips lightly graze my shoulder. Nothing out of the ordinary happens, but her touch makes me believe the sincerity of her words. Maybe Jadore is right: maybe Ms. Agailya has her own agenda, one that does not have the Collective's interests in mind.

Don't trust any of the professors, that's rule number two, Wil says. *But she may be right about getting to tutorial. We cannot afford to get on Jadore's bad side, not now.*

I nod and together we exit Rita House and head for MacLeod Hall. The corridor with the tutorial classrooms seems busier this morning, and I'm jammed against students of all colours and smells. I squeeze my eyes shut and pretend for one moment that everything is okay, and that last night did not happen, and that I'm just a regular freshman at a regular non-alien university. I put my trust in the flow of traffic to guide me to Room 216, where Jadore will be waiting.

Someone grabs my arm, and I come back to my senses. It's Wil. His eyes are sympathetic. *I know this is hard. I know you didn't ask to be involved. But our ability to survive depends on our ability to stay cool. Can you stay in control of yourself?*

I gulp and nod again. I don't have a choice. I have to keep my thoughts in the moment and put everything else out of my mind. At least, until this tutorial from hell is over.

Wil's thin-lipped smile is short-lived as he gently guides me away from the hectic flow of students to Room 216. The door is closed and Jadore is standing before the semicircle of chairs. My stomach sinks.

I can do this.

Wil opens the door, and the two of us step inside. The noise of the hallway drifts into the classroom briefly before Wil shuts the door again. Jadore stops her lecture midsentence. She doesn't turn her head. She's back in her human form—copper skin, conservative green business skirt and jacket, and a pressed tie the colour of her black-hole eyes.

Tap, tap, tap. Her walking stick is impossibly loud and echoey in the silent classroom.

"William McBride. Ingrid Stanley. You're late."

I swallow the words on the tip of my tongue: *You're not doing a good job pretending to be blind.*

Wil mutters an apology and takes an empty seat next to Jia. The only other empty seat is across the semicircle, away from my new friends. Jia's eyes widen at my presence, and she quickly averts her gaze, as if I am poison to look at. Misty snaps her gum and plays with her tongue ring. Some of the students look up at me from their notebooks, and I try to memorize their faces, because I chose their lives over Sunni's.

Cool. I have to stay cool.

I take a deep breath, sit down, and try to look inconspicuous as I rub at a dirt stain on my jean skirt. Great. I'm wearing the same thing as yesterday.

This is not going well.

Jadore taps her walking stick on the tile once more before she speaks again.

"I'm sure some of you may be wondering where Sunni Harris is today," Jadore says. Her voice is acidic, almost sarcastic. "A *wonderful* opportunity came up for her to study rare carnivorous plants at our sister school in the Philippines. She transferred late last night."

How can she just sit there and *lie?* Sunni died by Jadore's scaly, green hands—we'd all seen it! But none of the Sparks—not even Misty—react. They must have prepared each other for this day. The day when the Collective would catch one of them and break down their bodies for use in sick, alien experiments.

It's then it really hits home: there are no more empty chairs. I took the last free one. Every trace of Sunni is being erased from Sparkstone. No one is going to remember her in a few days. No one but us. And I'm living on what feels like borrowed time. *Who knows how long we've got to live.*

"The registrar's office is now open for transfer applicants. We have a variety of sister schools across the globe, each with unique opportunities in a number of fields. You can visit Ms. Agailya in her office to get an application, or more information." Her lip twitches into a smile. There are barely any laugh lines, or any other wrinkles on her face. "The deadline for transfers is the end of December, and each application is *thoroughly* considered."

The eight students in the tutorial who aren't aware of the Collective scribble this information furiously in their notebooks. I want to scream. They're *encouraging* Sparkstone students to be sent to their deaths. I wonder if the sister schools are even real at all.

"Ingrid? I don't hear you writing. Did you come to tutorial unprepared?"

I grind my teeth. I'd forgotten: my stuff is still in Ethan's locker. Even Wil has loose-leaf and a pen, presumably from the binder of paper Jia is writing on. Misty is doodling something on her left palm. I draw all of my anxiety into a deep breath and expel it from my body.

"Sorry. I . . . I forgot. I'm still learning the structure of these tutorials."

Jadore adjusts her large sunglasses, and I see my frightened reflection in them.

"Pens and paper, no laptops or other computers. Tutorials are meant to encourage inter-disciplinary discussion, to introduce and inspire ideas for the project within your majors. Have you given any thought as to what your majors and your project might be, Ingrid?"

My thoughts wander to the journal tucked beneath Sunni's pillow in her bedroom. Former bedroom. A bedroom that might soon be mine. Ms. Agailya's people have probably stripped the room of Sunni's belongings by now. That journal is probably being dissected right now by fishmen and whatever other weird aliens there are in the Collective. I should've taken it for safekeeping. Maybe that's what Sunni wanted me to do all along. I'll never know, now.

But whatever Sunni discovered through her dreams, it was enough to have her captured and killed. And if it has anything to do with the mysterious man whose face I know from somewhere unknown—the face that belongs to the name that terrifies Jadore—then there's really only one topic on which I can focus my studies.

"I thought what Sunni was saying yesterday about Joseph G. Campbell sounded interesting," I say, pronouncing each syllable as if it is my last. "So I'd like to do something on him. Not really anything from a theoretical physics perspective . . . maybe something from a psychological perspective. What effect the theory of multiverses has on the human brain."

Jadore's movements are slow. Calculated. She wraps one smooth, copper hand around her stick, and then another. She lifts her nose in the air, and then takes one careful step towards me. Her cheap plastic shoes give a dull *clunk* on the tile. She is not smiling now. "There is very little source material on Joseph G. Campbell for such an ambitious project."

"I'm not afraid of a challenge," I reply.

At this, she smirks. "No, I see that." After a tense silence, she continues: "If you are up to the task, there are a select number of tomes in the library that may be of some use to you. They are in the supervised, restricted area, but I could provide you access. In fact—there is no one better than myself to supervise this project. I happen to know a thing or two about Campbell's wilder theories."

Dammit.

I know nothing about Joseph G. Campbell, except what Sunni let slip in tutorial yesterday, and what glimpses I've seen of him in the last twenty-four hours. And I know that

Jadore hates him. Wil and Jia are staring at me intensely, as if warning me to back down. To stay cool. But it's too late for that. I'm in this all the way now.

"Talk to me after tutorial about this," Jadore says.

Tap, tap goes her stick on the floor. It's the sound of our impending doom.

She talks to the other students about their projects for about half an hour before dismissing the tutorial. Jia, Wil, and Misty are the first out the door. I want to flee with them. I stand like an old woman with unsteady hips.

Jadore is unmoving. She does not lean on her walking stick now. It does not tap. She holds it like a club. I take a step towards the door. Still, she does not react. If I ran into the hallway with my peers, she might not be able to catch me, not without exposing herself.

"You could've chosen the easy way, Ingrid," she says after a pregnant pause. "Music theory. Based on the quality of your audio files alone we could have lined up any prestigious performing artist to be your tutor in piano or Celtic harp."

Say nothing. I don't know whether the thought is my own or someone else's, but it is a good idea in any case. I purse my lips tightly and take another step towards the door.

Clunk, clunk. Tap, tap.

"I did not dismiss you yet, Ingrid."

You do not control me. I project all of my rebellious thoughts in one mental middle-finger gesture that I hope she can read.

She *clunks* and *taps* her way around me. I don't want to look at her, but I do. I don't want to be afraid of her, but I am. I am terrified. She could kill me with her stolen powers, with her DNA-infused technology. Instead, she raises a hand to her sunglasses. She doesn't take them off.

"The eyes are the hardest to hide," she says matter-of-factly. "We haven't developed the technology to modify them safely. Yet. But our organization has always found ways to take things and make them better."

There are so many things I want to say. So many things I want to ask her. So many things I wish I had never said in the first place.

"Don't underestimate my intelligence," she says tersely. "My hand has been stayed—for now. The moment you ripen, and slip up"—her snake-tongue slithers out of her mouth and across her lips—"is the moment when you and the rest of your friends join Sunni on the chopping block. I would opt to harvest all of you now, but the expense is much too great to harvest you individually at the moment, and we have to be sure that you're reaching your full potential before cutting you open. We're all waiting for *you*, Ingrid Louise Stanley."

My stomach turns. Still, I say nothing.

Then I realize. Jadore doesn't know that I teleported off the ship. She got away before we did. She probably thinks I teleported on the pads with Misty, Jia, and Wil.

She doesn't know I've already *ripened*.

"The rest of your time here can be pleasant," she continues as she strides towards the door. "Cause no trouble and your friends will live as long as my associates see fit. But if you attempt to meddle in our affairs again, or if you attempt to seek help outside of this town, or leave Sparkstone, I will terminate every human life-form in this facility." A sinister grin spreads across her face, and her copper skin becomes a venomous steel green. "Don't think I won't."

I pray she can't read thoughts. Just in case, I think of the most annoying tune I know and blast it through my brain. Jadore knows. She knows about me, about Misty, Jia, and Wil, and if any of us try to leave, everyone dies. I feel sick.

She fumbles for the doorknob and pulls the door open. "You are free to go now, Ingrid."

Except that I'm not. I stare at her, frozen with disbelief, before forcing my feet to move. Out of that room, out of this life, that's where I want to be. I want to be back in that moment where I thought I was in heaven with Ethan. The door clicks behind me, and even though I'm standing among my peers in a busy hallway, with the morning sun beaming through the six-foot-tall floor-to-ceiling windows, I feel her standing behind me.

Misty, Jia, and Wil are just a few feet away. Wil raises his eyebrows in a question that I'm afraid to answer. Should I tell them that Jadore knows? That the lives of our fellow students depend on our silence?

Misty already hates me enough. She'll find a way to blame this on me too. Wil and Jia might try to formulate some grand plan against Jadore and the Collective, which will only cause more trouble. But they deserve to know.

No matter what, I can't let any more of them die because of me. And whatever it takes, I can't let Jadore know that the Gene 213 superpower has already grabbed hold of me. This burden, just like the burden of knowing what was in Sunni's journal, and of recognizing the mysterious handsome man, will be my own.

But no matter what Jadore threatens us with, we will find a way to fight them.

"Hey, Ingrid, you all right there?"

Ethan's voice is a welcome distraction from my dark thoughts. I swivel around. His dishevelled hair clashes with the sleekness of his leather jacket, and his aftershave is inviting me closer to his skin. I grin up at him. He probably thinks I'm crazy. But yet, here he is.

"Yeah, um . . . I'm fine," I say. I shrug and pretend my thoughts are not serious. Especially my seriously hot thoughts about this morning, when I was even more of a crazy person than I am now. I shake my head. All of my thoughts lead back to Sunni's death and how I am partially responsible. "Sunni, you know, our friend Sunni? She was . . . transferred . . . last night."

"Transferred? Last night? I thought she was out with you lot."

"Yeah . . . she was . . . but then she had to . . . leave."

I chance a glance at my new friends. Misty is staring death at me. Black mascara runs down her face as hatred makes her lips tremble. I have no doubt that she can hear us.

Ethan follows my gaze. "She's taken it rather hard."

"They were good friends."

Misty storms off down the hallway. I watch her go because I don't want to look at Ethan and face the dreadful embarrassment that I know is going to come. I don't want to talk about this morning. I dig my fingernails into my skirt.

"I should really go. I still have to figure out my major, and get started on my—"

"Ingrid."

My name is soft and sweet on his lips. It wraps around my heart and stays my escape. I look up and he looks just as surprised as I do, but at least he has the courage to carry the conversation.

"I don't know what you were talking about out there in the field this morning, but if you're going to be transferred or leave . . . "

"Oh . . . I'm . . . not actually leaving." For a moment I consider telling him that that had been my plan all along.

"Yeah . . . I didn't think so." He half smiles. "I've had some pretty crazy nights, and sometimes when I wake up I'm so thankful that I didn't die of alcohol poisoning that I run around praising God too." He stuffs his hands in his pockets. "It's never made me brave enough to kiss a cute girl, though. That's a first."

I blush so hot I fear that my skin is going to boil. "I'm really, really sorry, I . . . I got really carried away. It won't happen again, I promise."

He looks disappointed. "Never?"

I think I'm going to cry happy tears. And then die for real this time. This is too much.

"How about, you take it easy today, and uh . . . " He hesitates and grins at my embarrassment, and then he's blushing too. "Okay. How about we, uh, get to know each other better? Wow, that sounded really, completely scripted. Let me try again." He clears his throat and then I'm giggling because really, everything about this is so absurd. He grips my hands and begs me to stop laughing long enough so that he can say, "You're a musician. I'm a musician. I play all sorts of things, actually. Guitar, violin, I dabble with the tin whistle. Let's get together for a . . . " He searches for a word that isn't *date*. "Jam session?"

I feel like a hot mess but it's okay. His hands on mine are what matter in this moment. "Sure. That sounds good." I squeeze his hands lightly. "Um . . . by the way, can I have my stuff back? It's in your locker."

"You remember the combo?"

"Yeah, I think so."

"Okay, good. I've got to get back to the studio, got a painting due this afternoon." He lets go of my hands and starts walking backwards and bumps into a wall of lockers. He quickly recovers, his face reddening. But at least he's still smiling. "I'll call you. Try not to reschedule this time, all right?"

Thoughts of last night's adventure invade my mind, and my giddiness, like Sunni's body, immediately vanishes. I draw a sobering breath and turn back to Jia and Wil. They're waiting for me down the hall. Sunni said that we have to protect each other. I try to take solace in that. But it's hard. It's really, really hard to be hopeful, when all I can think about is the lightning enveloping her body, bringing her to her knees.

"You're going to get us killed," Misty spits. "Joseph G. Campbell? Really? You might as well fall on a katana and offer yourself to the Collective right now if you're that stupid."

Back in Jia's dorm room, after any potential camera threat has been silenced, the mood is sombre. A large bowl of water sits on a chest at the foot of Jia's bed, and a dozen lit tea lights float on the surface. We have to do something to acknowledge Sunni, Jia had said, even if everyone else is going to forget about her. Think good thoughts about Sunni, remember the good times. The four of us hold lit tea lights in our palms as well, but no one is thinking about Sunni or any other good times.

"Jadore already knows about us," I reply. "She told me, after tutorial. She's watching us. And if we're not careful, she'll kill everyone in the school. Maybe even our families."

Jia shakes her head frantically. "No, no, she can't!"

"The more important question we should be asking ourselves," Wil says, casting a warning glare at Misty, "is why isn't she just killing us outright for knowing about the Collective's agenda, if she sees us as a threat."

"She's not the only one in the Collective," I say. "That mother ship is home to thousands of aliens. Who knows, maybe there're a million of them, swarming up there. The name in itself implies that there's at least a group of them making decisions. Maybe whoever is in charge of the Collective wants to keep us alive, for now."

"Yes, *for now*." The flame from Misty's tea light flares up to her eyebrows. "For all we know, Joseph G. Campbell is in charge of the Collective."

Wil looks thoughtful. "Maybe."

I shake my head. "I don't think so. But in any case, I now have an excuse to be close to Jadore. Even if she does know who I am, maybe I can try to get her to divulge information about the Collective."

And about Joseph G. Campbell and how I might know him.

Jia looks unsure. "It's so risky, Ingrid."

"I can handle it," I say firmly. "Do we know anything else about Jadore? Like what kind of alien she is?"

"Some kind of reptilian-humanoid," Wil says. "Like I said, this is the first time we've seen her true form. I sense . . . " He knits his eyebrows. "There's something off with her genetics. Like she's been modified in ways that can't be reversed. One thing I'm pretty sure about, her eyes are sensitive to our sun's light, so that's why she has to pretend to be blind."

"She's dangerous," Jia agrees. "The power she had . . . I don't even want to know how she got it."

"Probably from someone just like Sunni," Misty remarks.

"Stop it, Misty," Jia says.

Misty scoffs. "Why? You know it's true. They got Sunni. They know about us. They could be listening in right now."

"If they were going to kill us they would've done it the moment we landed in the shuttle bay," Wil says. "For whatever reason, we're more useful to them alive."

My mind reels with questions. "But how did they even find out that we had the gene in the first place? And is their technology so dependent on our genetic makeup that they need large quantities all the time to sustain their way of life? How long have they been harvesting people like this?" I think about Jadore's reference to the upcoming Harvest, singular, and my nerves twist into knots some more.

"These are things we all want to know," Wil says.

"I'm tired of waiting around. It doesn't matter why they're killing us. I'll kill Jadore first," Misty says. She has a dangerous look in her eyes. "I'll kill her, I swear it."

"We're not doing anything until Sunni is properly mourned," Jia says. "Sunni wouldn't have wanted us charging into their domain out of some selfish need for revenge."

"We can act out of justice."

Wil cradles his tea light in the centre of his palm. "I don't think that's what Sunni would've wanted either."

"Well, she's not here to tell us what she wants. All we know is that she was sure that Ingrid was important. And what does Ingrid have to show for it all?" Misty scoffs. "So she teleported off the mother ship. Could have been a fluke, or the alien wristband. Could she teleport somewhere if she wanted to? Does she have no control over her supposed powers? How do we know she's not working for *them*?"

Her last word is so filled with venom that I take a step back. "Look. I don't know if I have superpowers or a genetic mutation or whatever it is. It could've been the silver band—maybe yours don't have teleportation powers, but mine does. "

"You better goddamn well hope that you are one of us." Misty's fists are flaming red and blue. "Because if you're not, Sunni died for nothin'. And I swear to God or the devil or whoever is listenin' up there that if you turn against us, you will know what real pain feels like."

Her fist is so close to my face that sweat pours down my brow. "Misty, I would never—"

"Stop it. Don't call me that. You . . . all of you . . . my name is Mist now, okay? Only Sunni . . . " Her knuckles are white, she is squeezing her fingers so hard, and her face contorts into a sob.

"Misty, don't be like this," Wil says.

"I'll be whatever the eff I want!" Misty bellows. "This"—she gestures to the floating candles—"is stupid."

She whips around and heads for the door.

"Misty, please," Jia pleads.

"Don't," Misty warns. She holds up her fists. They burn red and glow blue. The tears brimming on her right eyelid freeze and drop to the floor while the tears flowing freely down her left cheek evaporate with a hiss. "*Don't* provoke me."

The door slams furiously behind her as she leaves. Jia

153

and Wil look awkwardly at each other as they place the tea lights on their floating holders in the pool of water.

"Shouldn't one of us go after her?" I ask.

Jia shakes her head. "Not when she's like this. It's too dangerous. She'll work it off. She'll mourn in her own way."

The heat from my tea light is soothing, and I think of Misty and all of her anger channelled into one flame. She had cried and cried as Sunni lay dying, and I wasn't able to help either of them. As I place my tea light in an empty holder in the pool, next to Jia's and Wil's, I vow that I will do what I can to help my new friends—regardless of whether I have special powers or not—so that Sunni's sacrifice is not in vain.

I'm packing a few things in my temporary room when there's a knock at the door.

"May I come in?" Ms. Agailya asks.

I open the door cautiously. She holds a wrapped package in her hands. "Sorry to bother you, Ingrid. This came for you this morning. I believe it's from your parents."

"Thanks," I say as she hands me the package.

I worry that she's going to stay and talk to me more, but she just smiles and closes the door. That's a relief. I wait a few minutes before slipping into the bathroom to open the package. I turn on the shower and run the sink to mist the mirror, just in case anyone is watching. Heat steams the room as I tear open the package.

It's not from my parents at all.

It's Sunni's notebook, the one that was hiding under her pillow. The one I read when I shouldn't have.

Is this some kind of sick joke? Are Ms. Agailya and Jadore going to come after me next? Fear grips my stomach and twists it as I flip through the pages. I turn over the book, and that's when I notice a Post-it taped to the back cover. The handwriting carries a hint of Celtic calligraphy, and the message sends chills from my ears to my toes. I gasp as I read it:

Keep this safe, lest it fall near unpleasant eyes. — J.G.C.

Joseph G. Campbell. So he really is trying to guide me. *Who is he, an alien? And is he really trying to help me?*

I lay the journal flat on its spine and it falls to the most-opened page. It's the sketch of the man's face. I rest my hand on it and my stomach tingles.

Sunni knew something about him that got her killed. Someone put the alien wristbands in the shuttle lockers. Either I had the power to teleport hundreds of thousands of kilometres, or someone saved me.

If Joseph G. Campbell is feared by Jadore, then maybe he's a friend, and maybe he can help us in our fight against the Collective.

But more importantly, he can tell me what it means to be the Crosskey.

EPILOGUE

Three times a day, Jadore lathers her face with the pale, cool cream. It sinks into her humanoid face—a face that she has come to admire, to accept as her own—with an intense, icy burning sensation. It tastes like peppermint. She knows the taste because the first few times she tried to ingest it, but then she decided she liked her tongue the way it was. Forked, split in two. How she survived with only that and her barbels to experience the world . . . well, it is hard for her to remember life before the Collective.

She sets aside the cream on the desk beside the rows and columns of monitors in the security room. They show only one scene. Misty Ellen Carter. Jadore uses the remote control to zoom in on her black-and-white tears. Misty is leaning with her face against a wall in Corridor H, in Rita House. Her hair covers most of her face, but the tears are slick and shine in the fluorescent light and leave traces on the off-white walls.

Jadore hisses with her human teeth. *Humans are one of the most wasteful species in the galaxy,* she thinks. *Spilling water with their eyes, throwing away precious resources, chasing fossils of dead animals to fuel their expensive, loud vehicles.*

Jadore's personal opinion doesn't matter to the Collective, so she only includes Misty's reactions to Sunni's death in her report. *Subject 3705-2 was particularly attached to Subject 3705-1. Her behaviour will be monitored for the next five rotations, as subject is prone to violent outbursts. Recommendation: isolate her from the others and perform amygdala scan, and up her Gen-Grow dose in her daily rations. Second recommendation: increase Gen-Grow dose in off-campus food. Third recommendation: put forward a motion to reopen the debate about Gen-Grow in Sparkstone water supply.*

The Gen-Grow in the food was her idea. So far, it has been the most effective way of encouraging Gene 213 to become a more dominant force within the subjects' bodies. The council hadn't always approved of Jadore's Gen-Grow initiatives, but that was before she replaced the third and fifth members with her men. Then she put the motion forward again, and it passed, barely, with a seven-to-six vote. Gen-Grow did not work on Ingrid Stanley, but creating a frequency with an alluring tune did wonders for the hafelglob bomb project. Jadore wishes she could take credit for the tune idea. Unfortunately, Campbell is always three steps ahead, and his ideas always sway the council in his favour. As long as the council remains under her thumb, and Campbell keeps his appearances at a minimum, she can continue operating the Sparkstone branch as she pleases.

The door to the security room opens. She smells the hafelglob in human form before she sees him.

"Good evening, Mistress," he says, bowing.

"You may revert to your natural form, Ohz."

He lets out a sigh, as if he's been holding his breath for hours, and balloons into his natural, blob-like state.

Jadore sets down her report. "Has the girl responded to your advances?"

A rumbling belly laugh erupts from his mouth. The hafelglob are known throughout the galaxy for their promiscuous behaviour, especially with other species. Most humanoids are disgusted by their appearance, but the hafelglob have proved very useful during the Collective's time on Earth. Best of all, they are loyal to her, and only her. Their demonstration with the explosives proved that. That little ruse was costly for the Collective and the hafelglob, and quite risky, but it proved that the hafelglob had the technical talents needed for the operation at Sparkstone. She would write another report and recommend that the hafelglob become full members of the Collective. The Collective would not be happy about the risks she has taken but they would commend her ingenuity. Testing for new memberships has to be vigorous and thorough, and Jadore believes that the bomb ruse was both of those things. Then, she can replace council members whose loyalties did not align with hers with loyal, obedient hafelglob soldiers. She would be more than just a modified face. She would rule them all.

"This one does not think the girl has what the Mistress seeks. But she is perfect specimen, as Sunni-girl predicted," he says, drool and spittle flying from his gigantic, slobbery mouth. Earth languages are sometimes messy for them to speak. "Crosskey smells like others with the gene, but . . . it is dormant, I think."

"Hmm. Then we will have to be patient. Her ability will awaken, as Sunni predicted." Watching Sunni's dreams was a nightly ritual for those on the Collective's council. A ritual that ended tonight.

The council will not take well to her death, Jadore thinks.

"The Crosskey will be more careful with her next move. We will continue to watch her, and the others."

"Council has not harvested others yet, Mistress?"

"They are too careful. Not every member is convinced the others show sufficient amounts of the gene to make the harvest worthwhile. Too many harvests would arouse suspicion." They can only explain away so many "transfers" to parents. Keeping up appearances is exhausting. There is no DNA cream for lies.

"Harvest completed on Sunni, though, Mistress," he says.

"Is it?"

So soon. The Collective employs the best surgeons in the galaxy. Of course they'd have cut Sunni open and harvested her genes for testing within the hour. "That is good news."

"Is," Ohz agrees. "Ready for next phase, Mistress?"

Her dark smile widens as she allows herself a celebratory swab of her genetic cream. Her skin absorbs it greedily. "Yes, I believe we are. Tell the council members I am calling a meeting. Tell them phase two is about to begin."

Acknowledgements

Once upon a time, no one ever read the acknowledgements page ever. This made the Acknowledgements Faery sad, and mad. So one day, she decided to take revenge on all book publishers everywhere. She cast a spell that made the acknowledgements page appear at random multiple times throughout the story, no matter what book you were reading!

Obviously this made a lot of people angry. *Death to the acknowledgements*, people would cry! But one brave soul stood with the Acknowledgements Faery: Sir Copy Right, a champion of the copyright page. He knew what it was like to be alone and unread, and always secretly loved the Acknowledgements Faery.

Will the Acknowledgements Faery find true love? Will the publishing industry ever be the same? I dunno, I guess you're just gonna have to read my next book and find out.

Champions of the Acknowledgements Page:

Jessie, Mum, Dad, Grammy, Grampy, Nanny, Poppy, Aunt Kerry, and family. Also: Marie & Joe Farrell, Rachel Small, and Chadwick Ginther. All of my Facebook and Twitter fans, you are, of course, champions as well.

And Dave, always.

About the Author

Clare C. Marshall grew up in rural Nova Scotia with very little television and dial up internet, and yet, she turned out okay. She has a combined honours degree in journalism and psychology from the University of King's College, and is a graduate from Humber College's Creative Book Publishing Program. She is a full-time freelance editor, book designer, and web manager and has clients all over the world. When she's not writing, she enjoys playing the fiddle and making silly noises at cats.

Photo Credit:
Terence Yung

Facebook: Facebook.com/faeryinkpress

Twitter: @ClareMarshall13
            @FaeryInkPress

Website: FaeryInkPress.com

If you enjoyed this book, please consider writing a review on Amazon or on Goodreads. Thank you!

Join Ingrid, Misty, Wil, and Jia in the next Sparkstone
adventure . . .

BOOK TWO
THE SPARKSTONE SAGA

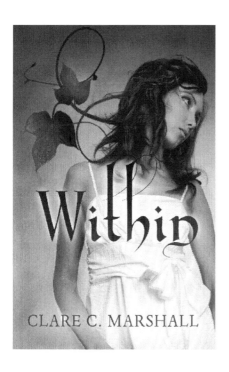

WITHIN
by Clare C. Marshall

$11.99
192 pages

YA Supernatural/Thriller
Ages 16+

ISBN: 9780987779403

Trinity Hartell's life changed after the accident. Left with irreversible brain damage, she becomes a burden to her mother, a cause for heartbreak for her boyfriend Zack, and a flattened obstacle for her jealous best friend, Ellie.

But then she starts writing. Perhaps it's a coincidence that the psychotic, murderous protagonist of her novel bears a striking similarity to the charming Wiley Dalton, a mayoral candidate in the upcoming election.

Or, perhaps not...

THE VIOLET FOX
by Clare C. Marshall

$20.95
288 pages

YA Fantasy/Adventure
Ages 12+

ISBN: 9780987779441

Run.
That's what instinct told me.
But to save the secrets of my people
and to protect my brother
I have to become the enemy.

There are two kinds of people in the land of Marlenia. The Marlenians, who live on the surface, and the Freetors, who are forced to live underground.

The war between them ended two hundred years ago, but the Freetors still fight for the right to live under the sun. Fifteen-year-old Kiera Driscoll embodies the Freetors' hopes as the Violet Fox. In a violet cape and mask, she sneaks around Marlenia City stealing food and freeing her people from slavery.

Then the Elders task her with a secret mission: retrieve a stolen tome that contains the secrets of Freetor magic, something the Marlenians both fear and covet. Kiera must disguise herself as a noblewoman and infiltrate the Marlenian castle before the Freetor-hating Advisor finds out her real identity, before her brother is imprisoned because of the secrets he hides, and before she falls any more in love with the prince she's supposed to hate.

More is happening in the castle than she realizes, and Kiera is faced with a difficult choice. Will she be loyal to her people and their fight for freedom, or will she be loyal to her heart?

39660479R00101

Made in the USA
Charleston, SC
17 March 2015